THE PINK SITUATION

COLORADO SPRINGS UNIVERSITY
BOOK 3

FELICITY SNOW

ACKNOWLEDGMENTS

A huge thank you to my amazing street team for helping spread the word about Chris and Paris's story. I couldn't do it without you guys!

Thank you to my amazing beta and sensitivity readers, Sarra Lancey, Hawthorne Grey, Erin Nelson, Rowan Oliver, Océane Anagonye, and Danielle Alana

And as always thank you to my editor Jen Sharon and my proofreader Becky Wenzel.

"I was made and meant to look for you and wait for you and become yours forever." Robert Browning

PROLOGUE

PARIS

A tear slides down my cheek as I stare at my phone screen yet again, reading the message for what seems like the hundredth time. I don't know why. I know what it says. Maybe I think it will help me process, maybe there's a part of me that thinks that maybe this time when I read it, it will say something else. Something that will make me smile or blush or laugh instead of making me cry. I mean, I know he wasn't marriage material or anything, (not that I'm looking for a husband at eighteen) but I liked him. And I thought he liked me. Also, I'm fully aware that I deserve someone who isn't going to break up with me over a text with nothing but, "Sorry, but it's not working out." So, yeah, it's not a huge loss, but it still hurts. Especially since I'm fairly certain I know what "it's not working out" is code for.

A shiver rolls through me and I curl into myself, wrapping my arms around my middle and pulling my sweater tight around me. It's March in Colorado, and right now it's freezing cold and snow covers the ground outside our cozy cottage style home.

It's beautiful. My parents had it built shortly after they were married and it's like something out of a magazine, surrounded by trees and nature, a gorgeous view of the mountains. In the spring, which will hopefully be in a few weeks, the land is full of wildflowers, and in the fall the trees are so colorful it's like living in a painting. The people inside are my absolute favorite. Right now Mom is puttering around the kitchen, Dad is probably snoring in his recliner with our dog, Ginger, on his lap, the fire roaring in the fireplace.

What's even better is that my big brother, Preston, is home right now for his spring break, and he brought his best friend, Chris, with him.

My chest squeezes when I think of Chris. His light brown skin, his tall, muscular frame, the way his warm brown eyes light up when he smiles and the way his rich, deep laughter soothes something inside me every time I hear it.

I've had a crush on my brother's best friend for two years, ever since Preston brought him home the first time. The worst part is, I know Chris will never see me the way I see him, because while I'm in love with Chris, Chris is in love with Preston. And Preston is clueless.

Up until this year, everyone thought Preston was straight, but then he met a guy in college, Jackson, who I guess made him go all heart eyes, and they've been obsessed with each other ever since. Honestly, Jackson is wonderful. I met him at Thanksgiving and he showed up for Christmas, too (right after he broke Preston's heart, though since his apology was pretty epic I have decided to forgive him).

Jackson isn't here now, though, because he's on a theater retreat of some kind with his classmates from college. Probably the only reason Chris agreed to come at all, because I know he would not want to be here if Jackson was here and he had to watch my brother and his boyfriend, uh, "interacting."

Anyway, I'm pretty sure the fact that Preston started dating a guy broke Chris's heart, but he'll never say anything to my brother because that's Chris. He's kind and thoughtful, and he wouldn't want to do anything that would make Preston uncomfortable or unhappy. And he knows Jackson makes him happy. All things considered I think he's handled it really well, but he hasn't gotten *over his feelings for my brother yet. And Chris has no idea that I know how he feels about Preston. Even when he showed up and Preston suggested they share a room, and a bed, and Chris's eyes were huge as he said he could sleep on the couch, Preston still didn't catch on. So I stepped in and said I'd share a bed with my brother and Chris could sleep in my room.*

Chris has only been here for five days of the two week break because he was working for part of it. But I guess he works so much his boss actually told him he needed to stop or he'd fall over dead and it would look bad for business, and made him take a break. I'm honestly not sure why, but Chris seems determined to get as many hours in as possible at the coffee shop he works at. I'm assuming it's got to do with paying for school, but I can't imagine he has much time for anything besides work and classes with how often he's there. And it's clear he's exhausted. Also, I'm pretty sure Preston said Chris is there on a scholarship. I mean, I know there are more expenses than tuition, but I honestly worry about how drained he seems sometimes, and I know Preston does, too, no matter how often Chris says he's fine.

I'm so lost in my thoughts that I don't notice someone has stepped outside until I feel a blanket being draped over my shoulders, and startle, looking up to find Chris smiling down at me before he moves to sit beside me on the front steps.

"Hey," Chris says, his voice deep and warm. His eyes dance over my face. "You okay?"

It's only then that I realize I still have tear tracks on my cheeks and hurry to wipe them away as I tuck my phone back in my pocket. "Yeah, of course," I lie.

"You've been out here for a while. And you looked upset when you left." I notice he's wearing a coat and hat, and normal people shoes instead of fluffy pink slippers like me.

God, why does he have to be so nice? So fucking perfect? It does not make my crush situation any easier, let me tell you.

I shrug. "Just high school stuff."

He gives a small smile. "High school sucks."

I let out a breathy laugh. "Yeah, tell me about it." It's not so terrible, honestly, especially since I have two amazing besties, but all things considered I'm definitely ready for it to be over.

"Almost done though," he says, nudging me. "Less than four months before graduation, right?"

"Yeah."

He ruffles my blond waves and smiles at me again. It's annoying and yet he's touching me, so I can never tell him to stop. I can never tell him it makes me feel like a little kid. That every time he does it it just cements the fact that he sees me as a little brother, and always will. "I came out to tell you that dinner will be ready soon."

Something about that makes my stomach sink. It's silly, because I should have known he didn't actually come out here to find me for the sake of checking on me, or spending time with me, but I could tell myself that was the case until now.

I sigh and feel another tear sliding down my cheek. I'm not really even sure why. But I don't try to hide it this time.

"Hey, come on, Pip," Chris says, draping his arm over my shoulders. "Whatever it is, it will be okay."

A shiver races down my spine when he tucks my head against his shoulder and his fingers skate up and down my back over the blanket he gave me. He chuckles, probably assuming the shiver is from the cold. God, he's never been this close to me, and everything about it is amazing. The way he smells like Mom's snicker doodles, and the warmth radiating off of him. The way I can feel his breath on my hair. His hand as it moves to my shoulder, strong and steady and reassuring.

"Why don't we go inside and get you warmed up?" he says. "I can make you some hot chocolate."

My heart squeezes and I lift my head, my gaze meeting his. The sun is setting over the mountains now, the cold air biting at my face. My toes and fingers are numb. But his eyes are soft, and warm, and even on his tawny brown skin I can see the hint of rosiness on his nose and cheeks as his breath ghosts over my face, his fingers moving up to skim over my neck.

He's so close, and I want him so much, and I feel sad and hurt, and despite being surrounded by my family, I also feel alone. And he *makes me feel safe and good and warm. So, even though my brain is screaming at me not to, telling me it's a terrible, horrible, no good, very bad idea (yes, I loved that book as a kid), that it could and probably will ruin everything, I find myself leaning in and pressing my lips to his.*

ONE

PARIS

Fuck, okay, here we go. It's going to be fine.

"Hey, you okay, squirt?" Preston asks, resting his hand on my shoulder as I stare at the apartment building I'm moving into, my hands gripping the handles of my very large, very full, bright pink suitcases which are housing my most essential items: make up, hair products, skin care, my five (I was going to bring more, and forced myself to leave some behind) favorite purses, nail supplies, and jewelry. I have a separate suitcase just for shoes. My clothes are in a separate suitcase as well, also pink. But they don't need to be handled nearly as carefully, so here we are.

It's only a few more days until classes start and I'm officially a college freshman. Honestly, it's a little scary, but mostly exciting. I'm looking forward to meeting people, starting my psych classes, and getting the full college experience. The best part is, my best friends Vanessa and Trent are here, too, so we'll still be close to each other. I'm majoring in psychology, Vanessa is an education major, and Trent is a computer science major. They've been my besties since sixth grade and have been there for me through all the shitty moments in my life. I don't know what I would do without them.

For example, they're the only ones who know that I kissed my brother's best friend six months ago, and that I'm also moving in with him.

Today.

Right now.

Cue twink panic. Yeah, that impromptu kiss, shock of all shockers, didn't go well, at all, and I can't tell anyone else about it. I can't tell my parents or Preston that I can't live with Chris because I'm a fucking idiot who can't keep his emotions in check and made my brother's best friend super uncomfortable to the point where he looked at me like I'd zapped him with a stun gun, proceeded to mumble several incoherent words, and then bolted. Like literally, he was gone the next morning (after a super awkward dinner). When I asked what happened, Preston said Chris's boss asked him to come back early and pick up a few more shifts at work, which I know is a load of baloney. And I'm not sure Preston believed it either, but I sure as hell wasn't going to volunteer any information. But I knew. I'd freaked him the fuck out.

I fucked up, big time.

And then, shortly after that debacle, my parents and Preston suggested that since Preston was moving in with Jackson, it would work out perfectly for me to be Chris's new roommate. Since he didn't veto the idea I assumed he hadn't wanted to say anything about the kiss either.

So, here we are. And I haven't seen or heard anything from Chris since that day. But it's fine. I'm totally fine. Completely and utterly fine. I didn't know my body was capable of producing this much sweat, and like, ew. My heart is beating so fast I might pass out, I feel sick to my stomach, and I'm honestly surprised I haven't peed myself, but I'm fine.

"Paris?" I blink out of my anxiety riddled daze and look at my brother. He's wearing the same purple baseball cap he always wears, along with a loose fitting tank and shorts. He's the typical jock. Tall, muscles, lots of tattoos, and then there's me. I'm none of that. I'm short, slender, five foot four (and a half, thank you very much), and dressed in white skinny jeans with holes in the knees and a bright blue cropped T-shirt with Care Bears on it. My sneakers have glitter on them, my nails are pink, and I don't have anything resembling muscles anywhere on my body. Instead of tattoos I have glitter eyeshadow and strawberry lipgloss. The only thing that's the same about us is our eye color–blue, and our blond hair.

I love him to pieces, though. The best part about my family is that they accept and love me for exactly who I am, and I know I'm safe with them. They're my fiercest supporters, defenders, and encouragers, and it means the world to me. I wasn't always comfortable with being this version of myself. In fact it took me a long time to embrace the real me, but I'm here now, and I'm never going back. I know my parents are worried about how people will treat the very gay, very fem twink, which they've worried about since I was a kid, but they also know it's important for me to spread my wings. And the fact that Preston and Jackson, and Chris and my friends are here I think eases their concern a bit, too.

"Yeah," I say, forcing a smile. "I'm good."

"Great, let's get this show on the road," Preston says, grinning at me. He moves to the car and starts grabbing things out of the trunk as Jackson, his boyfriend, steps up next to me, a large box in his arms. He's dressed in black skinny jeans, a black vest, no shirt underneath, and his black hair looks almost bronze in the sunlight. One thing I love about Jackson is that he also wears make up. Not as much as I do, but he has this really amazing smoky eyeshadow that he taught me how to do and the eyeliner he wears makes him look surprisingly badass. He's incredibly slim, with a runner's build, and wears even more jewelry than me, though his is a bit more goth or rockstar and mine is, well, feminine. Whereas I enjoy wearing pearls and heart necklaces, he has black and silver earrings in each ear, and large rings in the shape of animals decorating his slender fingers.

He nudges me. "You're gonna be great," he says in his deep voice. "Come on."

I take a deep breath and nod, and we make our way up the steps and inside the building.

CHRIS

Jesus Christ, I've never felt so fucked up in all my life. I've been cleaning non-stop for the last two hours. I've wiped the kitchen counter down fifteen times. I've vacuumed, dusted, scrubbed the toilets, mopped the floors. I even took the time to clean out the refrigerator. Not because I felt like it, not even because it just needed to be done. No, I'm on a cleaning rampage because that's what I do when I'm stressed. I guess you could say that having Paris Wright as my new roommate after what happened over spring break is freaking me out just a little, but I also knew I couldn't say no when Preston's family suggested it. I couldn't tell them what happened, but I also knew I needed to stop running from my problems and face them. And now I'm wishing past me had been a little less mature because present me is a wreck.

Ideally I'd be at work right now, but of course, I don't go in until later this afternoon, and I could pretend to be busy somewhere else, but I feel like ditching my best friend and his little brother while they move Paris's things in, when I don't actually have anywhere else to be is a little dickish.

I'm fluffing couch pillows for Christ's sake. I don't fluff pillows. I don't even know where these pillows came from. But I have to do something or I'll lose my mind. If it wasn't for my music I'd be even more of a mess than I already am. I'm a huge fan of Brittney Spencer. There's a softness, vulnerability and soulfulness to her music that captures me and always makes me feel a little bit more grounded, and listening to her while I clean is helping some, thank god.

I should be going downstairs and helping everyone bring Paris's things in, but I can't bring myself to do it yet. I'm stalling as long as I can before I have to see him.

Seconds later, though, time is up and Preston is opening the apartment door. I have my laptop out on the kitchen table, though I'm not actually doing anything on it, when I see him, Jackson, and finally Paris, enter.

"Hey, we're here," Preston says, grinning at me. I smile back at him as I stand and turn off the music on my phone. I make eye contact with Jackson, who nods at me, before my gaze meets Paris's for only a second and then darts away again. I shove my hands in the pockets of my jeans.

"Great, you guys know where the bedroom is. If the car is unlocked I'll go down and grab some things."

"Go for it," Preston says, then moves towards the bedroom, Jackson and Paris following. Fuck, I know we're going to have to face each other eventually, or living together for the next year is going to be hella awkward. Right now, though, avoidance is my strategy.

It takes about twenty minutes of all four of us going back and forth to get all of Paris's things inside. His room is pretty much bursting with boxes and luggage and I'm honestly not sure if he actually left anything at home. He's got a decent sized closet here, though, and he's using Preston's old bed, dresser and desk.

I drop my last box off and scurry away into the living area like the scaredy cat I am. I ran into Paris a couple times on the stairs but we ignored each other like all mature adults do, and now I'm pacing around the kitchen.

Realizing how exhausted and hot I am after the manual labor, I reach in the fridge and grab some water bottles, setting them on the counter and helping myself to one. I'm chugging like my life depends on it when Preston and Jackson join me.

Jesus, it pisses me off that I still get flushed at the sight of Preston in his ridiculous tanks, sweat dripping down his chest. That my heart rate picks up whenever he smiles, and that my stomach fills with butterflies at even the lightest touch from him. I've been in love with my best friend for two years, and he doesn't have a clue.

Seeing him come to terms with his own sexuality and start dating another guy was honestly one of the hardest things I've been through. There were nights where I just sat in my car outside the apartment sobbing because I knew he was in his room getting fucked by Jackson and it made me sick to my stomach.

But I didn't begrudge him his attraction, or his happiness, and I knew that no matter what, I wanted him in my life. So I sucked it up, and tried to be the best friend I could be for him, to love and support him, even though everything in me ached for him to look at me the way he looked at Jackson, to smile at me the way he smiled at Jackson, to see his golden skin flush when he was with me the way it did when he was with Jackson.

Seeing their relationship progress was both beautiful and gut-wrenchingly painful. Because I knew Jackson was it for him. And while I had my reservations, especially after Jackson broke his heart last year, I've grown to respect and appreciate him more the longer we've known each other. I know he loves my best friend more than anything, and that he's working on the things that hurt Preston in the past, so yeah, I can't even bring myself to dislike him.

I think my feelings for Preston have dulled some, which I'm thankful for. I'm realizing he was never meant to be mine, and I'm slowly starting to be okay with that.

"Water?" I say, gesturing to the bottles on the counter. Preston grabs one and hands one to Jackson.

"You guys gonna be cool?" Preston says as he leans against the counter and drinks.

I nod, feeling my cheeks heat. "Yeah, of course. Why wouldn't we be?"

He shrugs. "Just, look out for him, huh? He seems nervous. I mean, he's stupid smart, and I know he's gonna do great, but . . ."

I nod again and squeeze his shoulder. "Yeah, of course. You know I will."

Preston nods.

"You guys want lunch?"

"No, thanks, we're meeting up with Rory and Parker for lunch," Jackson says.

I nod, wishing I could think of anything to say to keep them here so I can go on not facing Paris. But alas, I have nothing, so I have to watch them walk through the living area and down the hall to Paris's room. They're back in a second and heading for the front door.

"We should hang out soon," Preston says when he hugs me. "For real. Let me know when you have a free night."

"Yeah, I will." I work so much that when I'm not in classes or doing homework I'm at the coffee shop, so free nights are rare for me, but since classes don't actually start for a few more days, my schedule is a little bit more open at the moment. "Actually, I'm free tomorrow night after my shift."

"Awesome, let's do it. I'll bring a pizza over or something, yeah?"

"Sounds good."

He claps me on the shoulder and heads out the door with his boyfriend.

I sigh and turn to see Paris standing in the kitchen, a water bottle in his hand, his eyes on me, and biting his lip. He looks as nervous as I feel.

In fact, in all the time I've known Paris, I don't think I've ever seen him so visibly uncomfortable. He's usually so full of life and energy. Always ready with a sassy comment or a sarcastic remark. Always radiating confidence. Now, though, he looks . . . anxious, and maybe even a little scared. And yes, while I wasn't thrilled with the kiss six months ago, I never want him to feel like that, especially not around me.

He clears his throat. He fiddles with a bracelet he's wearing, pink of course. Paris loves pink. And it's difficult to tell from this far away but I'm pretty sure it has unicorn and rainbow charms dangling from it. Like always, his blond waves are artfully tousled, his make up is pristine, and his clothes fit him like a glove, the pale blue cropped shirt with the Care Bears falling just above his belly button ring, and the white distressed skinny jeans clinging to his slender legs and the curve of his ass. He's . . . I'm not sure there's a word in the English language that is accurate for describing Paris's breathtaking beauty. He's stunning, captivating. But even those words don't do him justice. High cheek bones, full pouty lips, pale skin, and striking blue eyes give him an almost fae-like appearance, minus the pointy ears of course. I've always thought Paris was beyond gorgeous, objectively speaking that is.

"Hey," he says softly, and gives me a little awkward wave that is so un-Paris like it makes me crack a smile. I step closer.

"Hey," I reply, hands tucked into my pockets. "How are you feeling about everything? I mean, being away from home and starting college, and all this." I wave my hand around the apartment. It's simple, the living area and dining area are open concept and the two bedrooms are on either side, nowhere near each other, thank god, because listening to Preston and Jackson go at it was not on my bucket list. We each have our own bathrooms, too, which is nice.

Paris shakes his head, setting down his water bottle. He folds his arms over his chest. My brows furrow when he says, "Don't do that."

"Do what?"

He glares at me. And for some reason it makes me chuckle, and some of the tension in my shoulders eases. Because that glare is all Paris.

"Pretend like nothing happened. I know I fucked up."

I shake my head this time. "It's okay–"

"No, it's not," he says, his voice stern and his face flushed, whether from the exertion from earlier or from being upset, I'm not sure. "Just please, let me say this."

I nod.

"I shouldn't have done what I did. It was wrong. It was stupid and selfish and immature and so fucked up. I put you in a really uncomfortable position and made things really awkward for you, and I'm really, really sorry. I know you don't feel that way about me, and I respect that, and I promise it will never happen again. And if you don't feel comfortable with me being your roommate I totally get it and I will go inform Trent that I'm crashing on his dorm room floor for the foreseeable future because as terrible as that would be, it would be far less humiliating than telling either Preston or my parents what happened and why I've been kicked out of your apartment. Of course I'd probably have to leave my things here because I wouldn't have room for them at Trent's, but I can figure something out. Maybe I can sell everything and use the money to pay Trent for his floor space, or I could live out of my car. I mean, I don't think I'll be nearly as pretty after slumming it but–"

I'm laughing now, as I step forward and cover his mouth with my hand. "Stop," I say as his eyes widen. "You're not going anywhere, your things aren't going anywhere. I accept your apology. We're good. Yeah?"

He nods and I move my hand, then hold it out. "Friends?"

He grins and places his tiny pale hand in mine. "Friends."

TWO

PARIS

Fuck, that's over, thank god. I honestly thought Chris might hate me. Was there a small part of me that was secretly hoping he'd tell me he'd actually enjoyed the kiss and was pining over me for the past six months and had realized how in love with me he was? Yes, of course, but this is good. We're friends, and as crazy as I am about him, I can do friends.

I know people have unrequited crushes and feelings for other people all the time. It's nothing new, and I'll get over it. Eventually.

"You must be hungry," Chris says.

"Oh my god, I'm starving," I say, placing a hand on my stomach as it growls.

He chuckles. "I can make us some sandwiches. You like turkey?"

"Yeah, sure, but that's your food. I should get my own. Add that to the very long list of things to do, I guess."

"It's fine. I don't mind sharing." He gives me that amazing Chris smile, the one that makes me turn into a puddle of goo every time, and I sit at the table sipping my water while he puts two sandwiches together.

"You like mustard?" he asks, looking over at me.

I wrinkle my nose and he laughs again. "I'll take that as a no."

"So," he says, joining me a moment later and sliding a plate across to me, a yummy sandwich with turkey, cheese, lettuce, tomato, mayo, and no mustard on it, along with a handful of chips, "same question as before. How are you feeling about all of this?"

"Pretty good, I think," I tell him, then take a bite of the sandwich. "I mean, I'm a little nervous, but I'm excited, too. Ready for a new chapter in life. I think I'm more worried about my parents than I am about myself. I know being empty nesters is hard on them, especially Mom, and after everything with Phoenix . . . " I trail off as thoughts of the older brother I lost invade my mind. God, I miss him. Every single day. I was in middle school when he died and it destroyed me. He was my hero, and the main reason I felt brave enough to finally come out and be myself after so many years of hiding who I was.

I feel a warm, soft hand squeezing my forearm. "It's scarier for them to let you go," Chris finishes my sentence for me. I nod. Mom had a really hard time letting Preston go to college two hours away, but she managed and he's done great. Though she does call several times a week to check up on him. After Phoenix had a seizure and drowned on a school trip she had a harder time letting either Preston or I out of her sight. She's made progress, though, over the years, and she knows we need our freedom and independence, but she worries. And I know her and Dad both worry more about me because I'm small and gay and fem, and it makes me a target for bullies. Not that I haven't dealt with my share of that over the years. Never any physical violence, but I've been called all the names and been treated like garbage, and I've learned to ignore it because I like who I am, and I know the only reason people harass me is because they're afraid and they don't like who they are.

"Your whole family has been through a lot," Chris says, his voice gentle, hand still on my arm. "One thing I know though, is that through all the shit storms, you love each other so much. And I know you're going to do amazing here."

I smile. "Thank you. That means a lot." He's right, too. Not only did we lose Phoenix, but the very next year, Mom and Dad both got diagnosed with cancer. Fuck, it was awful, being so young, having already lost my big brother and being terrified of losing my parents, too. I was so grateful for Preston during that time. He was so strong and he kept me from crumbling to pieces so many times. So did Vanessa and Trent. I don't know how I would have made it through without them. I can't tell you how many nights I couldn't sleep because I was so scared and stressed and they stayed on the phone with me, or even spent the night at my house all cuddled up with me in my double sized bed, just holding me. Fortunately, Mom and Dad are both cancer free now.

I take another bite of my sandwich and wash it down with a gulp of water, then ask, "How's your family doing?"

He moves his hand from my arm and I miss the touch immediately. He gives a small smile. "They're good."

I don't know a lot about Chris's family. I know they live in Minnesota, that his dad's name is Luke and his mom's name is Tawnya. I know his dad is a mechanic and his mom is an artist and that he has two younger sisters, Janelle and Ruby. He doesn't talk about them a lot, but from what I've heard they sound great. Supportive, kind, loving.

"They're cool with you being gay, right?" I ask, when he doesn't volunteer anything more.

"Yeah, they're great with it."

"How old are your sisters now?"

That makes him smile a little more. He clearly adores his siblings. "Janelle is fourteen and Ruby is ten."

"I bet your parents have their hands full," I say with a grin.

"Yeah, they're good kids, though, which helps. Especially with . . . " he trails off and I wonder what he was about to say, but I don't press him. I wonder if it's related at all to why he works so much. I can tell the topic is making him uncomfortable, though, so I change the subject.

"You got time to help me with my room or do you have plans?"

He gives me a relieved smile. "I'm all yours for the next hour, and then I need to get ready for work."

"Let's go then, handsome. Your twink dictator awaits."

He chuckles and follows me to my bedroom. Honestly, I know I packed a lot, and looking at how full the room is is kinda overwhelming, but it's essential. Yes, I did need to bring all the artwork for my walls, and my fluffy pink pillows and my curtains, and I may have packed a few different hair dryers, because what if one breaks? And yes, I do need all of the shoes, and no I don't think an entire suitcase (it's small, okay?) of pretty panties is over the top.

Chris clears his throat. "Where do we start?"

"You can do shoes." I point to the contraption lying on the bed with a bunch of different pockets in it. "Hang that on the back of the door and then fill it up. Shoes are in there." I point to one of the many pink suitcases I brought.

"Only one suitcase for shoes?" he teases as he maneuvers his way through the boxes and luggage.

"I was forced to downsize," I pout. "And I'd rather not talk about it if you don't mind, I'm still processing the trauma."

That makes him laugh and I grin. Making Chris laugh and smile is number one on my list of hobbies.

While he's working on the shoes I busy myself with unpacking all of my clothes and hanging them in the closet.

"You wanna listen to music?" I ask.

"Sure."

"What do you like?"

"I was just listening to Brittney Spencer. She's one of my

go-to's when I'm doing chores or exercising. I also love Tracy Chapman, but she's more for relaxing or when I'm doing homework. But we don't have to listen to either if you want something else."

I grin, because I love that he shared that little snippet about himself with me. "I'm not familiar with either, but I love trying new artists." I look for Brittney Spencer on my Amazon music app and press play. Not long into the first song I decide I definitely want to hear more, and I understand why Chris loves her so much. Her music is soulful and her lyrics are deep, but fun and flirty, too. And her voice is soothing.

It doesn't take long for Chris to get the shoes situated and then he's asking me what's next. "You can unpack the rest of the clothes," I tell him, motioning to the other suitcases. "All of that stuff can go in the dresser." I have my tops and skirts in the closet, but the jeans and pajamas can go in the dresser. Along with the socks and tights.

It's not until he's clearing his throat and I turn to see a faint blush creeping up his tawny cheeks that I realize, right, that's the suitcase with my, um, unmentionables. Panties, to be exact. Lots of panties. And a few bralettes.

"You want me to . . . " he trails off, and it's difficult to tell, but I think maybe his blush is deepening. Honestly it's kind of adorable, seeing him all flustered. I'm not shy about that kind of stuff, though, so him seeing my panties or touching them doesn't bother me. It's just underwear. We all wear them. And he's going to see them in some capacity if we're living together.

"If you want to leave the panties for me that's fine."

He clears his throat again. "No, it's okay, if you're okay with it, I mean."

"I'm fine with it. You can put them with the tights and socks."

He nods and gets to work. I hope I haven't made him uncomfortable, but he didn't have to do it.

Just to be safe though, when I finish up with my task I say, "Hey, why don't I take over there while you hang my curtains for me?" I hold up the pink tulle curtains and give him a megawatt grin. He does seem a little relieved to have a new chore, but when he takes the curtains from me and I move to the dresser I see that not only did he unpack all the panties, he has them stacked on top of each other neatly, unfolded, in a few different piles, and that he made sure the tights stayed folded neatly when he transferred them. The fact that he took such care with my things means a lot to me.

I hear him messing around with the curtain rod while I gather the pants out of my suitcase and slide them in a separate drawer, and then, because I have quite a few pajamas and some of them take up a fair amount of space (they're the big onesies) I leave the rest of the drawers for those.

When I'm finished, I look up and see that the curtains are hanging and look amazing, and that Chris is holding up a few other large pieces of pink tulle fabric with a quizzical expression on his face.

"What's this?" he asks.

"That's my bed canopy from home. I don't know if it'll work to hang it though since we can't drill anything. I wanted to bring it just in case because it's my favorite part of my bedroom. Well, other than my dressing table which I couldn't bring, but if it doesn't work it's okay. That's what the fairy lights are for, too."

"I think we can figure it out," he says, "but maybe not right now. We'll probably need a few things first."

"It's fine, really. You don't have to figure it out, it's not your job."

He frowns at me, but then says, "Anything else?"

"You wanna help me hang some stuff on the walls?"

"Of course I do."

For whatever reason that makes me smile. Chris is the most kind and selfless person I know, and I'm honestly loving getting to spend this time with him.

"I think there's some 3M stuff in the hall closet we can use so we don't put a bunch of holes in the wall. I'll be right back."

CHRIS

Okay, that was . . . unexpected. I mean, am I surprised to learn that Paris wears pretty bras and panties? No, not at all. Am I surprised to learn that my dick likes that Paris wears pretty bras and panties? I'm honestly trying not to think about it. Or that fact that I was getting harder and harder with each item I picked up and placed in his drawer. Jesus, what the hell is wrong with me? He's my best friend's little brother!

Okay, breathe. People see other people's pretty lace bikinis and sheer thongs every single day, right? It's normal. It's . . . fuck, it's hot as hell. And honestly, the scariest thing is that I haven't been aroused by anything in a long time. I've been too busy and too stressed to even contemplate having sex, and I've been too fucking exhausted to even pleasure myself most of the time. But touching Paris's lingerie woke my libido up like nothing else.

Jesus Christ, I'm fucked up. It's Paris! Best friend's little brother! Not cool.

Okay, I should have been back with the supplies I'm gathering a long time ago. So I take a few more breaths, think of all the reasons my life sucks, and yep, that does it, my dick is flaccid again shortly.

I return to the room with the necessary supplies, and Paris and I work together on getting all the art that was in his bedroom at home, on his walls here.

I'll admit it was hard seeing Preston move out, even helping him pack and seeing how empty his room was, knowing I wouldn't be living with him anymore, but having Paris here is honestly really nice. And I'm enjoying helping him make the room his.

There's a picture of the Eiffel Tower and the word Paris across it that he directs me to place above the head of his bed. The black and white photos of a high heeled shoe and a pair of lips go on the wall above the desk.

Paris tosses his pink bean bag chair in the corner and then proceeds to unbox some stuffed animals and arrange them around the bean bag chair.

His phone buzzes and he takes it out of his pocket. "Ooh, yes."

"What's up?"

"Oh, Trent and Vanessa want to meet up for coffee and then go bowling. And I'm dying to get out, so perfect timing. I'll get to the rest of the unpacking later."

I chuckle. "Makes sense, you've been cooped up here for almost two whole hours."

He grins at my sarcasm and winks at me.

"Well, I gotta get ready for work, so I'll see you later?"

He nods. "Thanks for everything. You're amazing."

I ruffle his hair and leave the room to get ready for my shift, telling myself that I am NOT wondering what his little bubble butt might look like in those sexy as hell panties.

THREE

PARIS

"So, tell us how it's going so far," Vanessa says as she sips on her mocha frappacino. Her dark curly hair falls to her shoulders, framing her olive skin and her green eyes peer at me inquisitively. One of the things I love about having Vanessa as a friend is that she's not afraid to say it like it is. She's also the same height as me, which makes me feel less pint-sized.

"It's been two hours since I moved in," I remind her. Vanessa is living with her two older sisters in an apartment near campus and has been settled for a few days already, while Trent just arrived this morning to meet his roommates and get situated in his dorm. His parents came with him to help get him settled, took him out to lunch, and then headed back to the hotel they booked for a nap. He looks exhausted and it's only two in the afternoon. Vanessa on the other hand, is bright eyed and bushy-tailed.

"Yes, and how did it go? Did you guys talk? Was it horrible? Details, girl."

"It went better than I expected," I tell them. "I apologized for the kiss. He was super nice about it, and then we had lunch, and he helped me unpack. That's it."

"That's it, huh?" She waggles her brows.

"Stop, you can't do that," I tell her, slapping her arm playfully. "I need to get over him. Don't encourage me."

"He helped you unpack?" Trent says in his deep, raspy voice. He's average height with ivory skin, a slender build, but still more toned than me. His wavy brown hair falls over his forehead and a dusting of freckles decorates his nose and cheeks. A pair of black framed glasses are perched on his nose as well. Typical nerd, but that voice has gotten him lots of dates, and hookups, let me tell you.

I shrug. "He's nice. He was being a friend."

"Uh huh," Vanessa chimes, taking another sip of her drink.

"Honestly, guys, please don't make this something it isn't. I've already fucked it up enough and I just want to be his friend now. That's all."

"Okay," Trent says, his hands in the air in the familiar backing off gesture.

"How's your roommate?" I ask him, taking a swig from my caramel iced coffee.

He shrugs. "He's fine. Straight, though, I'm pretty sure, which is a pity."

Vanessa and I both laugh and Trent gives us one of his rare grins. He's generally pretty stoic and really doesn't emote much but he will when he's with us. I consider it a privilege. He's bisexual, as is Vanessa, and has the most boring wardrobe I've ever seen. Jeans and T-shirts, my friends. It doesn't get much worse than that. He's cute, though. I think it's the glasses that really do it for him. And the voice. Did I mention the voice? Sadly, he's not my type, but he's super smart, and one of the kindest people I know. And when I was really struggling in middle school with figuring out who I was, he was there for me. They both were. They were the ones, other than my brothers, who encouraged me to dress the way I really wanted to but had been scared to for fear of being bullied. And when I finally did it, and wore a skirt to school, they gushed over how proud they were of me. Vanessa glared daggers at anyone who tried to look at me funny and Trent threatened to hack into their phones and computers and subsequently destroy their lives if they so much as made a single rude comment.

After coffee we head to a nearby bowling alley where we eat way too much pizza and popcorn and drink an ungodly amount of soda. We laugh as we talk and share stories, and we get a little crazy with our bowling moves, and I don't think I stop smiling the entire time.

That night when I get home I realize I haven't actually made my bed yet, so I throw on some sheets and my white comforter. I drag the empty boxes to the dumpster outside and tuck my suitcases in the closet. Finally I can breathe in here, and it's looking really nice.

I get my toiletries and make up situated in my bathroom. I really am bummed I couldn't bring my dressing table with me, but it would have been a pain to transport and it wouldn't fit in the room anyway.

Chris is still at work even after I shower and change into my pajamas; short shorts and a cropped camisole. I'm realizing we should probably exchange numbers so we can keep in contact now that we're roommates.

And since I have to be at freshman orientation tomorrow morning, I decide it's time to put my cute little twink butt to bed.

I spend the next day touring campus, meeting with my academic advisor, attending information sessions, registering for classes, and of course, joining the LGBTQ club, which sounds amazing.

It's late afternoon when I finally get a break and decide I need to do some grocery shopping. When that's accomplished and everything is put away, I shower and get ready to head back to campus for the event the LGBTQ club is holding for the incoming freshman.

I'm walking into the living room, ready to grab my keys and leave again when Chris comes through the door. It's only then that I realize I haven't seen him since yesterday afternoon, and fuck, he looks exhausted. I wish I knew what to do, how to help him.

"Hey," he says, giving me a tired smile when he notices me. He kicks off his shoes and tosses his keys in the bowl by the front door. "You heading out again?"

"Yeah, LGBTQ event on campus for us newbies."

He looks me over a little and his smile gets bigger. "I like your outfit."

I'm wearing a rainbow skater skirt, a black cropped tank top, black tights, bright pink ankle boots, and a necklace with my name on it. My belly button ring is a rainbow. I also have loads of bangle bracelets decorating my wrists. And to top it all off, black and pink smoky eyeshadow. I'm also carrying one of my favorite purses. It's black, except for the corners which are pink, and it has a bow on the top on each side. Super cute, if I do say so myself.

"Thank you," I say, with a flourish. Then add, "Hey, I was thinking maybe we should exchange numbers."

"Mmm, yeah, good idea," he mutters, sauntering over to the sofa and collapsing on it.

"Were you at work this whole time?" I ask him, sitting on the couch and pulling my phone out of my purse.

He nods and I nearly gawp. I mean I know he slept, but then he got up and went back to work at like seven in the morning. He was gone when I got up, and he's just now getting home? Jesus. No wonder he's exhausted.

"Here, give me your phone," I say, holding my hand out. He does and I enter my number before handing it back to him. He types something on his phone and a second later mine buzzes. I pull it out and see the new number and the message. It's just a simple *Hi*, and a smiley face, but somehow it makes my heart flutter.

"You should get some sleep."

"Probably, but I'm hanging out with Preston tonight. And I might need that more."

I nod. "Well, I hope you have fun."

"You, too." He gives me another tired smile and I stand, grabbing my keys and giving him one last look before heading out the door.

CHRIS

"So, how's living with Paris been so far?" Preston asks as he stuffs his face full of the pepperoni pizza he brought.

"Fine. I haven't actually seen much of him. I have a feeling it'll be that way in general with my schedule and how much he likes to be out."

Preston chuckles and takes a swig of his soda. "Probably. He can't sit still for two seconds."

I smile, then blush when I remember helping him unpack yesterday and the effect it had on me when I saw all of his sexy lingerie. Still trying not to think of that, by the way. God, if Preston knew I had had any thoughts involving his brother and lingerie, he'd kill me.

"How are things with Jackson?" I ask, desperate to get my mind on something else.

Now it's apparently Preston's turn to blush, and I immediately regret the question. "Okay, never mind," I hurry to say, taking another bite of my pizza. "I don't want to know."

He laughs. "We're good," is all he says, but he has that adorable mega watt smile on his face.

"You guys gonna come to Jackson's play in November?"

"He's in it?" I ask.

"I mean, not yet, since auditions aren't til Monday, but I'm sure he will be." Last year Jackson was Dr. Frank-N-Furter in

The Rocky Horror Picture Show, and yes, he was incredible, I have to admit. Preston took me to see it and it was amazing.

"Do you know what the play is?"

"Nope. Something classic, I think. But honestly, it doesn't matter, because if Jackson's in it I know it'll be amazing."

I laugh. It's sweet how supportive Preston is of his boyfriend, vying for people to come see a show when he hasn't got a single detail yet.

"Paris should come, too."

"Hell, yeah, he should. We can all go together."

I nod. It'll mean missing out on a work opportunity, or precious hours I'll need for studying, but I don't want to let Preston down, or miss a chance to hang out with him. And I love theater, so it'll be good for me.

There's a pause before Preston says, "You okay? You look exhausted, man."

"I'm fine," I tell him.

"You have circles under your eyes."

"I'm fine," I repeat, more aggressively.

"Look, I just worry about you. You're working yourself too hard. It's not healthy. I know you worry about your family, and your mom, but they wouldn't want you to kill yourself trying to make things easier for them."

My jaw clenches. "I'm fine."

Preston sighs. "How is your family?" I know he's concerned about me, but I've been doing the job and classes for a year and a half now. Yes, it's a lot with all the hours I'm trying to work, but I know what I can handle and I've got it under control.

"I don't know," I tell him. "I mean, they don't talk to me about their finances, but I know it's tight. Mom is okay. She's got good and bad days. She's working some, but not as much as she would like to, and my sisters are wanting to do more and more extracurricular activities. Besides, I'd really like to try and make it home for Christmas this year."

"I know," he says. "I'm sorry things are so hard. I know

what it's like to have parents who are sick and want to help, to do what you can to make the situation better. I know you feel helpless, but you can't keep burning the candle at both ends. You know that's not what your parents would want."

I tighten my jaw. "Drop it, Pres. I know you want to help, but it's my family and my choice."

He sighs, but doesn't say anything else. I hate that the evening has taken such a shitty turn already. I want to enjoy this time with him, not spend it at each other's throats.

"Did you get the text from Parker about the get together at his and Rory's place next week?" Parker is a mutual friend of ours, and he's dating Rory, a friend of Jackson's. They're about as opposite as Jackson and Preston, but they're adorable together. Parker is bigger than me, and all muscle, and Rory is the size of Paris. He's a cute little nerd with freckles and glasses.

"Yeah, for Rory's birthday?"

I nod.

"Yep, Jackson and I are both gonna be there. You coming?" The way he says the last part is so hopeful it makes my chest ache.

"Planning to."

That makes him smile.

"Want to help me with something?" I ask, standing to toss my paper plate in the trash and taking his with me.

"What?"

"A super simple project that will make your brother very happy."

He grins. "Of course."

After we finish with our project, Preston joins me on the sofa for a couple episodes of *The Good Place*. It's one of my favorite comfort shows and I got him hooked on it a couple of years ago. It never fails to make me laugh no matter how many times I watch it, except for the last two episodes which never fail to make me cry.

I don't honestly have a lot of time for television, especially once classes start, but I try to get at least an episode or two in a week because it really does help with my stress level and letting me unwind.

After a couple of episodes we switch to video games, and by the time he leaves, I am well and truly exhausted, but in the best way.

FOUR

PARIS

When I get back to the apartment it's after midnight. Preston's gone, and most of the lights are off, including the one in Chris's room, which I'm thankful for. I hope he sleeps for twelve hours straight.

Tonight was fun. Vanessa and Trent were there, too and we had a good time playing games, doing ice breakers, and getting to know the other freshman and the upper classmen who lead the LGBTQ club. There was yummy food and at one point we divided up into teams to do queer trivia. It was awesome, and I got a lot of compliments on my clothes and make-up. Being around other queer people just makes me happy. The authenticity, the joy, the knowledge that we're all coming from the same place even though our stories and how we got where we are are different.

I mosey through the living area, smiling at the signs of Chris and Preston's evening together. An empty popcorn bowl, Nintendo Switch controllers on the coffee table, soda cans, a half empty–or half full I guess–bag of Doritos. As I move closer to my room I notice that even though the light is off there's still a faint glow coming from inside, and when I reach the doorway my hand flies to my mouth and goddamn it, tears fill my eyes.

That big, beautiful man hung my bed canopy, and it looks amazing. The faint light is because he also decorated it with the fairy lights I brought with me from home. More fairy lights decorate my curtains.

Goddamn it, he's amazing, and I hate him. He can't do stuff like this and expect me to get over him any time soon.

I turn on the lights to see how he did it. There's command hooks and curtain rods above the bed and the different pieces of pink tulle fabric that make up the canopy hang from them. It's not the same as it was at home, but it's beautiful and I love it. I might love it even more just because he did it. I mean, I probably could have done it, maybe figured it out for myself at some point, but I'm the least handy person in the world, so the fact that he just did it because he knew it would make me happy? Fuck.

I move towards the bathroom with a ridiculous smile on my face, and it doesn't leave even while I brush my teeth, remove my jewelry and make-up and pee.

I change into my bunny footie pajamas, and crawl under the covers of my gorgeous bed, feeling cozy, safe, and happy.

When I wake up it's bright outside and the sun is streaming through my bedroom window. A look at my phone tells me it's almost eleven. I stretch and take a few moments to appreciate my canopy yet again.

When I hear noise in the kitchen I jump out of bed and scurry down the hall.

Chris is there, a cup of coffee in his hand, dressed in pajama pants and a black T-shirt, looking semi human for once. He still looks tired, but not deathly so. He grins when he sees me.

"Good–" he starts, and then lets out an "Oof," when I envelop him in a hug. "Jesus, Pip, careful. I almost spilled on you."

Oh, fuck, he used the nickname he gave me when we first

met. Well, it was Pipsqueak first, but he shortened it a while ago and he hasn't used it since I moved in. Granted, it's only been a couple of days, but I missed hearing it so much. I thought I might have screwed things up so badly with that kiss I would never hear it again. My stomach flips and I squeeze him tighter, laughing when he grunts.

"Thank you," I tell him. "It's beautiful and I love it and you really shouldn't have because you were so tired already, and you're so sweet. Thank you."

He chuckles. "Preston helped."

"Oh, fuck I have to pee. Be right back," I say and scurry away, grinning as his laughter bounces off the walls.

CHRIS

I honestly can't remember a time when I smiled as much as I have the past couple of days. Something about Paris just makes my heart happy, lighter. He's so full of energy and life it's contagious, and I don't feel as discouraged when he's around. And fuck, why did having him in my arms feel so good? So . . . right? I shake my head, dismissing the thought.

When he returns to the kitchen a moment later I'm at the stove scrambling eggs and I've got toast in the toaster.

"You want some?" I ask.

"Ooh, yes please." He hops up on the counter next to the stove and grins at me in that ridiculous, but yes, completely adorable bunny onesie, complete with the hood with bunny ears attached and the tail. And yes, I may have caught myself staring at his ass when he headed for the bathroom. Seriously, though, the fluffy bunny tail is right there.

"Nice jammies," I say with a grin.

He beams and it's the cutest thing ever. "Thank you. I also have a penguin onesie, a koala bear, a unicorn, and a monkey. But this one is my favorite." He wiggles his butt on the counter and I chuckle.

And then, before my brain can catch up with my mouth I

say, "You do make a very cute bunny." My cheeks heat but he just grins wider and then hops off the counter to get the toast and some coffee for himself while I plate the eggs.

While we eat he tells me about his night with the LGBTQ club, the activities they did and the people he got to know. I've never been one for spending an evening talking to strangers, but Paris loves meeting new people and having new experiences, so for him, it's perfect, and I'm glad he's finding ways to get involved on campus and do something that matters to him.

"I was thinking," he says around a mouthful of eggs. "Would you be okay with me sprucing up the apartment a little bit?"

I blink. "Sprucing it up?"

"Yeah, I mean, just some color here and there, maybe a few decorations? It's so boring in here it makes me sad." He pouts and I can't help chuckling.

"Sure, why not?"

"Yay!" he squeals and wiggles in his seat, and I laugh again.

FIVE

CHRIS

"Ahh, yes, I'm so glad you're here." Parker gives me a huge hug, practically squeezing the life out of me as he lets me in the door of his apartment. "Help yourself to food and drinks in the kitchen. And make sure you stay for at least half an hour. It's important." He grins so wide I think his face might split. Parker is the sweetest guy on the planet. We got to know each other through being in a lot of classes together and other than Preston, he's my best friend. I do feel bad I don't get to see more of him but my schedule is so packed it's hard for me to find time for friends. And I can't slouch when it comes to my classes and grades either because I'm desperately hoping for a scholarship to grad school.

Preston and Jackson are here, mingling, as are about a dozen other friends of Parker and Rory's. There's birthday balloons, a Happy Birthday banner, and streamers. Parker finds me a few minutes later in the kitchen, filling up a plate with snacks, and holds up a birthday hat, beaming at me. I groan and let him slide it on me. He's wearing one, too, and looks absolutely ridiculous but also unbelievably excited.

"You're awfully happy," I tell him, and his grin gets even wider, his cheeks flushing. I raise an eyebrow. "Any reason?"

His eyes widen. "Uh, no, of course not. Maybe. I mean, yes, but it's a surprise." He mimes zipping his lips shut and scuttles away. Okay, then.

I make my way into the living room and find Preston and Jackson among the crowd. "What's up with Parker?" I ask. "I mean, I know it's his boyfriend's birthday, but does he seem even more . . . Parker-ish than normal?"

Jackson chuckles and takes a sip of his drink. "He's definitely got something cooked up."

I spot Rory across the room talking to his friend, Lucy, and he has a flush on his cheeks and a big grin on his face. He's dressed in his signature chino pants, dress shirt, suspenders, and bow-tie and I have to admit, he looks pretty adorable.

He's not one for big crowds. Parker's told us he gets over-stimulated really easily so I know the party won't last long, but he seems like he's enjoying himself for the moment anyway. I don't know him really well, but I do know the guy he was dating before Parker was a total asshat. Cheated on Rory on his birthday last year in fact, so I'm sure this is Parker's way of showing Rory how much he deserves and how special he is.

We talk and eat, and about twenty minutes into the celebration we sing *Happy Birthday* to Rory (quietly, while he flushes adorably and buries his face in Parker's chest), and then my eyes widen when Parker takes Rory's hand in his and gets down on one knee.

"Holy shit," Jackson breathes. He catches Lucy's gaze across the room and she's crying. I stare as Parker pulls a ring out of his pocket and holds it up. The room is completely silent save for some gasps, sniffles, and squeals.

"Oh my god," Rory whispers, his hands over his mouth as tears slide down his cheeks. He squirms as Parker holds his hand and looks up at him.

"Freckles," Parker says, and everyone chuckles and

"Awws" as Rory flushes even deeper, bouncing on his toes. "I love you so much–"

"Yes!" Rory squeals, and there's more fond laughter when Parker grins like a lunatic.

"I haven't asked you yet," he teases, and Rory bites his lip, squirming some more.

"Sorry."

Parker winks and then continues. "Meeting you was the best thing that ever happened to me. You're the cutest, sweetest, smartest, most amazing person I know, and I adore every inch of you. You make my life better in every possible way and I want to spend the rest of my life loving you. Will you marry me?"

Rory nods frantically, tears spilling down his cheeks and squeaks out, "Yes."

The room erupts in cheers and applause as Parker slides the ring on Rory's finger and then stands, taking his much smaller boyfriend . . . fiancé in his arms and lifting him. Rory's legs wrap around his waist as they kiss.

Wow. I'm so fucking glad I didn't miss this. They're so damn happy and they deserve every moment of their joy. I can't believe I got to be a part of their engagement.

"Well, fuck, that happened," Jackson says, then discretely wipes a tear from his eye before we all go over to congratulate the happy couple.

"That was one hell of a surprise," I tell Parker, slapping his back. And of course, because he's Parker, he pulls me into a bone crushing hug.

———

When I get home that night it's late, but despite that I feel better than I have in a while. Probably because I was able to relax and unwind and spend time with my friends. And because seeing two people so happy and in love is pretty magical.

Yeah, I'm a bit of a romantic. Maybe it's because my own parents are so in love with each other after being together for twenty-five years that I've grown up believing love really is possible, and that loving the right person makes you better. Not perfect, of course, not that love is a cure all, but that being with someone who knows you, who challenges you and encourages you, and adores you, who sees your imperfections and flaws and loves you anyway for just who you are, makes you capable of being the best possible version of yourself.

The apartment is dark and Paris is asleep, so I try to stay as quiet as possible as I make my way to my own room and get ready for bed.

I pop my earbuds in and turn on Tracy Chapman because thinking of my parents makes my thoughts drift to Mom, and I always heard Tracy's music coming from Mom's art studio whenever she was working. She introduced me to Tracy Chapman and I've grown up listening to her music. She still listens to her on a regular basis and I have fond memories of her singing along while she painted or baked, and my parents dancing to her songs each evening after dinner.

My chest aches at how different things have been the past several years, but I try not to dwell on it as I brush my teeth and use the bathroom. My family has been through a lot but one thing I am always thankful for is how much my parents love each other, and how close we are. I miss them. Being away from home for months at a time is rough, even though I love my classes and the friends I've made here.

I change into pajama pants and a T-shirt, and crawl into bed, thinking of home and letting Tracy's folky music put me to sleep.

———

It's not until I've stumbled out of bed the next morning and poured myself a cup of coffee, that I turn and nearly choke on said coffee at the sight in front of me. Our dining room window, which was previously void of any decor, just an empty curtain rod hanging over the blinds, is now draped in a set of very pink curtains.

Fuck. My eyes land on the pink vase decorating the dining room table. It's filled with pink and white artificial flowers. Above the dining room table are three large pieces of artwork. One says "Love" in HUGE all pink letters. One says "Do what makes you happy" in smaller font, and the third is a giant pink feather.

There are pink and white seat cushions on the chairs, and as I step into the living room my mouth falls open. The sofa is covered in a pink slipcover, and pink and black pillows in the shape of hearts and flowers sit on top. There's a very fluffy pink blanket draped over the armchair.

Holy fuck. I know I said Paris could spruce up the apartment, but I honestly was not expecting this. I'm going to get so much ribbing from the guys if they step foot in here. It doesn't look bad, it's just very VERY pink.

I sigh. Very very Paris. It looks like Barbie and Valentine's Day had a baby, and that baby threw up in my apartment. Ugh.

Just as I'm thinking that maybe I should talk to him about toning it down a little, maybe making it a little less pink, everywhere, he comes bouncing into the room in his fluffy pink bathrobe and slippers, his eyes bright and a huge smile on his face.

"Ahh, you saw it! Isn't it gorgeous? I just love it. I had so much fun. Thank you for giving me free reign by the way. I already texted pictures to my mom and she loves it."

I zip my lips and ruffle his hair. Because there's no way I am going to kill that contagious enthusiasm. If he loves it so much, who am I to complain?

"It looks great, Pip," I say, and am rewarded with that breathtaking smile.

Okay, so I am not saying anything to Paris, but I do decide to text Preston after Paris leaves for class because I have to groan/complain to someone.

Your brother decorated our apartment, I text, then insert several photos. His reply comes seconds later.

Woah. That's a lot of pink. And hearts. Cringy face emoji. Did he do that without talking to you? Sometimes he gets so excited about things he doesn't think about that kind of stuff.

Alas, no, I told him he could spruce the place up. I guess I just wasn't expecting this.

Lol, you mean Barbie's dream house? he replies, and I laugh.

Exactly.

You could always ask him to scale it back.

No, I can't. You should have seen his face this morning. He was so happy. I'll survive.

Lol, you're a good guy, Chris. I'm glad he has you.

I tuck my phone away and get ready for class. It's going to be another long day. Class and then work, and if I'm lucky, I'll find time to study. Though what I really need, if I'm being honest, is a nap.

PARIS

"Tell me again why I'm letting you paint a dragon on my face?" Trent says in his sullen voice.

"I told you, I need practice," I say, brushing the orange paint over his forehead.

"You paint things all the time," he points out, holding his light brown waves off his head, his glasses in his other hand.

"I paint nails. Not faces. This is new for me, and I don't want to fuck it up."

It's been three weeks since classes started and the college is hosting their fall festival in a couple of days. The LGBTQ club is going to have a face painting booth and asked if I'd be interested in helping. They'll also be giving out information packets, free stickers, and rainbow bracelets. Since the LGBTQ clubs I was a part of in junior high and high school were so instrumental for me, I said I'd love to help. And because my friends love me, they got roped into helping me practice. I've been painting designs on people's nails for years and I'm getting better and better, but painting a much bigger design on someone's face is a bit more intimidating and requires a bit of a different technique.

"Hold still you whiny baby, I'm almost done," I tell Trent.

"My arm hurts from holding the hair out of the way for so long," he grouses.

"I can pin it back with a pretty pink bow," Vanessa chimes in, and winks at me. I laugh and Trent snarls.

"No bows. And no pink."

"What did pink ever do to you?" I say.

"Pink is great," he deadpans. "Just not on me."

"Boring," I say with a sigh.

"Oooh, it looks so good," Vanessa squeals when I'm finally finished.

I smile, because it does look pretty good. Especially for my first try.

"Okay, let me see and then I'm gonna wash it off," Trent says, reaching for the mirror Vanessa is holding out.

I gasp. "You will not be washing it off. Not after all the blood, sweat, and tears I put into it."

He glares at me and I pout. "Please? Leave it on for at least an hour?" I bat my eyelashes at him and he groans.

"Fine." He looks in the mirror and I catch the faintest hint of a smirk on his lips.

"Told you it was good," Vanessa tells him. "Now move your butt. It's my turn."

SIX

PARIS

The campus is alive with activity. Since the Fall Festival is a community event there's tons of people here. College students of course, families with small children, even non college students here on dates.

There's different booths set up, like the one I'm working, a whole slew of carnival games, an apple bobbing station, hayrides, inflatable bounce houses, slides, and even an obstacle course and pumpkin painting, as well as a few other crafts. There's also a photo spot decorated for the season with a line a mile long. Food trucks are lined up and there's cotton candy and popcorn for sale. It smells amazing and my stomach growls.

There's even a stage in the center of the quad where different college groups are performing. There's dancing, singing, and even some skits taking place.

I've been at my station for about an hour and the line for kids and even some adults who want to get their faces painted is never ending. I honestly didn't expect it to be this busy, but I'm enjoying myself, chatting with my "clients" as I do my best to give them the design they want.

Fortunately I'm not the only one here. There's another student, a sophomore that's involved in the LGBTQ club who has a station next to me so we can get to the guests faster, and there's two more students sitting at the table with the rainbow tent over it, talking and engaging with anyone who wants more information or just to chat.

"You're doing really well," Trinity says from her spot next to me as I work on finishing up the butterfly the little girl in front of me asked for.

I blow out a breath. "Thanks, I've been a little nervous."

"Don't be. It looks like you've got a real talent for this stuff." She's currently painting a unicorn on the face of the little girl seated opposite her.

"Okay, you ready to see it?" I ask my young client. She has dark hair, golden skin and the sweetest smile. She nods eagerly and I hand her the mirror. She's shrieking as she jumps off the stool she was sitting on and wraps her arms around me.

"I love it, I love it, I love it! Thank you! Also, you're super pretty and I love your skirt." She grins and waves and then runs over to where her parents are. They smile and wave, mouthing "Thank you" before they walk away.

Trinity chuckles. "Told you. Also your skirt is super cute. I love how you dress. And you need to show me how to do my make-up so it looks as amazing as yours."

I'm grinning from ear to ear and not at all paying attention to who my next client is, instead watching as Trinity finishes up with the little girl in front of her, so I nearly jump out of my skin when a deep voice says, "Hey, there."

I manage, barely, not to shriek as I put my hand to my chest, catching my breath. When I turn to face my client he's grinning widely. "Sorry, gorgeous, didn't mean to scare you."

I flush. He is really cute. Pale skin, jet black hair, and a sexy as fuck smile. He's bigger than me. I mean, everyone is bigger than me. Close to six feet and a decent amount of muscles. They're hard to miss since he's wearing a tank top. I'm honestly kinda surprised to see him here. He really doesn't seem the type to want to get his face painted.

"Uh, it's fine. I'm fine," I stammer, my cheeks heating. "You uh, you want anything in particular?"

"Your number?" he says, then winks at me. My eyes widen.

Oh.

Oh.

I'm speechless. And then someone slaps me. "Ow," I say, turning to glare at Trinity who gestures at me in a way that says, *Fucking say something to him.*

"I um, I don't think so," I say. "I don't know you and this really isn't a good time."

"Fair enough," he says, not really fazed at all by the rejection. "I'm Jeremy." He holds his hand out and I shake it.

"Do I get your name?" he asks, when I just sit there like a dumbass.

"Oh, right. I'm Paris," I say, realizing I still haven't stopped shaking his hand. I blush again and let him go.

"Well, it's nice to meet you, Paris. I don't suppose you get a break any time soon?"

I debate whether or not to be honest with him, but I don't see the harm, so I say, "In about fifteen minutes, actually."

He grins, and yeah, it's really hot. Fuck. The problem is, I've been here before. And it never works out because none of the guys I'm interested in want the same things as me. And I'm tired of feeling like it's my fault for wanting something they don't. For being someone they don't expect.

Still, I can't sit around pining for my roommate endlessly, and he's being nice enough.

"I'd love to buy you a coffee, or anything really, if you want to meet me over by the picnic tables when you get done here."

I swallow. "I'll think about it."

He stands and winks at me again. "See you soon, beautiful," he murmurs, then walks away.

I'm distracted as hell for the next fifteen minutes,
wondering what just happened and trying to decide if I'm
going to meet up with Jeremy or not.

"Girl, if you aren't going to go find that gorgeous hunk of
man then I will," Trinity tells me, and I laugh.

"You like girls," I point out, and she shrugs.

"I mean, I'm pretty sure, but he's making me second guess
myself," she says, and I laugh again.

In the end, I do decide to go find Jeremy by the picnic
tables. It's a short walk across the quad before I reach the
area. There's several food trucks set up and several picnic
tables in the center filled with people eating, drinking, and
chatting.

I spot him sitting at a table scrolling on his phone. He
grins when he looks up and sees me walking towards him.

"Glad you came," he says, standing. "You want a drink?
Or a snack? I'm sure you're hungry."

"Um, that's okay, you don't have to buy me anything." I
decide the best way to face this is head on so there's no confusion and no mixed signals, so I blurt, "If you're looking for a
hookup I'm not your guy. I don't do one night stands."

He's silent for a moment, just staring at me, then, "Good
to know. I'll be honest, I was kinda leaning that direction, but
I'm cool with just talking and getting to know each other a
little. Taking it slower if that's what you need. No pressure if
you decide you hate me."

I bite my lip, trying not to smile. The tension leaves my
body and I start to relax. Okay, so that went better than
expected. Maybe this time is different? Maybe this time I
won't be pushed into doing something I'm not ready for and
don't want.

"I wouldn't say no to a hotdog," I say, and he grins.

———

"Hey, there's my baby boy," Mom says, smiling at me through the phone. "How are you doing? How are classes?"

"I'm good. Classes are going well." I talk to my parents about once a week, though I know Mom would talk to me every day if she had her way. I fill them in on my comings and goings, my involvement on campus, the different events I've been to or been a part of. I assure them that I'm fine. That I'm safe, and happy. I haven't told them about Jeremy yet. It's only been a week since we started going out, and I like him, but I'm not ready for that conversation, especially since I have no idea where it's going. He's been great so far. I mean we've only officially been out once since the festival, and he joined me for a game night with the LGBTQ club. For our date he took me to a movie and then we walked around a nearby park. It was nice. We held hands, and he kissed me goodnight when he dropped me off. It was a sweet kiss, no tongue, and it was pleasant, I guess, but no fireworks or anything. Not like the way my body lit up from the inside out when I felt Chris's lips against mine for the brief second that lasted.

But Chris isn't an option. Sigh. I want to give Jeremy a chance, though. He's been patient with me, gentle, and hasn't pushed for anything more. He's honestly really easy to talk to and he makes me laugh.

"Hey, bud," I hear Dad's voice and then his face enters the screen and he's smiling, his eyes bright. My parents are in their sixties now and both retired since they were older when they got married and had children. God I miss them so much all of a sudden.

I mean, I love being on my own and figuring out life as an adult. But my parents are amazing and they've always had my back. If it wasn't for them I don't know how I would have gained the confidence to be the real me. They never asked me to hide my love of skirts and dresses, or make-up, or lace, or pink. Mom was always happy to let me try on her shoes and jewelry, and always let me paint my nails with her. They let me explore and discover and figure out who I was without criticism or judgement and I blossomed because of it. They let me show them who I was instead of telling me who to be. Not saying it wasn't super hard some days to embrace myself and all my uniqueness, but they were there for me through everything. Through all the tears, and anxiety, and frustration, they were my safe space, and I'll always be grateful for that.

I miss Mom's cooking, and Dad laughing as he sits in front of the TV watching reruns of old 70's shows. I miss the smell of cinnamon that always invades our house and watching *Star Trek* as a family. I miss the easy way we banter back and forth during meals, and shopping trips with Mom. And I miss my dog. Ginger is a miniature labradoodle. She's blind and deaf but still hanging in there at sixteen years old. She spends most of her time curled up in her bed by the fireplace or on Dad's lap. I'm honestly kinda terrified she's going to die while I'm in school and I'll be a mess. She's been with us since she was a puppy and I was really little, and she's the best dog in the world.

My chest aches as I look at them, the pride and joy on their faces evident, and tears start to fill my eyes.

"Hey, what's wrong, kiddo?" Dad asks.

"Nothing," I say, wiping my eyes and laughing a little. "I'm fine, really, I just miss you guys, and I don't know how I would have made it this far without you."

"Oh, honey," Mom coos, "you know we love you more than anything in the world. We're so proud of you every single day. And being your parents and watching you grow into who you are, that's our privilege. You're so brave, sweetheart, and so beautiful inside and out."

"Okay, you're not helping with the crying," I mumble, and they laugh a little, though Dad has tears in his eyes now, too. He's always been a softy. I guess that's where I get it from.

"Hey, can I say hi to Ginger?" I ask.

"Oh, yeah, of course," Dad says and disappears.

"You're really okay?" Mom asks, and I nod.

"Yeah, Mom, I promise. I really am. I'm staying busy, but I'm good. It's a great school, I've got my friends, and Chris is the best roommate, though I hardly see him, to be honest, he's so busy all the time. And I've really enjoyed being involved in the LGBTQ club. We had a barbeque the other night that was really fun."

"I'm really glad to hear that, baby," she says.

"Hey, girl, it's Paris," Dad says, now back on the screen, holding Ginger in his arms. God, I'm emotional today because the tears start again as I wave at my blind dog, and say hi to her knowing she can't see or hear me. But somehow she must sense something because she starts wagging her tail and her ears perk up. I wish I could reach through the phone and pet her.

"Okay, maybe that wasn't such a good idea," I say, wiping more tears from my eyes. Ginger is my girl. Growing up and knowing I was different from the other boys in my school was hard. So fucking hard. It involved a lot of internal battles and acceptance to get where I am, but Ginger was always there when I was upset or scared. She let me hug her and cry and she licked my tears away so many times.

"She knows you love her, bud," Dad assures me. "I'll give her lots of cuddles for you tonight."

"Thanks, Dad."

"You know you can call anytime no matter what," Mom tells me.

"I know," I say. "I love you both."

"We love you, too," she says. "Bye, baby."

"Bye." I wave at them and end the call, then realize I only have an hour before I'm supposed to meet Trent and Vanessa at Rave, the local LGBTQ club. We can't purchase alcohol since none of us are twenty-one, and we have to wear special colored wrist bands that say so, but we can still dance and enjoy good food, and get non-alcoholic drinks, and just enjoy a fun place to unwind with other queer people.

I dress in black leather pants that hug me in all the right

places, a black cropped button up tank top with a collar, and biker boots, but just to add some color I do pink eyeshadow and some glitter on my face. Then I add a pink heart belly button ring and top it off with my bright pink vegan leather jacket.

When I step into the living room I see Chris coming in the door. We've lived together for weeks now and I see him less than I see Vanessa and Trent. Far less. We're rarely home at the same times and when we are he's locked away in his room studying, or asleep.

"Hey, Pip, you look good," he says. "Heading out?"

I nod. I want to preen at his praise but I can't because he looks so miserable and his voice is laced with exhaustion.

"There's some pasta in the fridge," I tell him. "I made some for dinner and you're welcome to have the leftovers."

"Oh, wow, that's amazing. You're sure?"

"Of course." I give a small smile. "You gonna relax at all?" I could stay home just so I get the chance to see him. But what's the point? He'll be doing homework anyway.

"Probably not. I've got a paper due soon and reading I'm behind on."

"Well, text me if you need anything," I say, though I'm not sure what that would be. And I'm pretty sure I'm the last person he'd ask for help. I know Preston has tried to get him to cut back on the work hours. No one can work a forty hour week, be in classes full time and not collapse. But I know telling him to take it easy won't work.

At least I could help him by having some food ready when he got here. I decide that even though it's not much, my new goal is to make sure dinner is ready when he gets home so he at least doesn't have to worry about cooking and can get some protein and carbs in him.

"Have fun," he tells me as he saunters towards the kitchen.

I wave and head out the door.

Rave is amazing. Lively music, great food, and though Trent is not a dancer at all, Vanessa never hesitates to join me. It's just what I need to relieve some stress.

After eating and spending some time on the dance floor I return to the booth the three of us snagged when we came in. Trent is on his phone, Vanessa is dancing with a cute girl, and I find my thoughts drifting to Chris again. When my phone buzzes my first thought is that maybe it's Chris reaching out. I'm surprised to realize I'm disappointed when I see it's Jeremy.

I smile though when I see his message.

Hey, gorgeous, can I take you out tomorrow night?

Sure, I reply. *What did you have in mind?*

They're showing a movie on the quad. It's gonna be a little chilly but not too bad. I'll pay for the popcorn, smiley face emoji. 7 o'clock

Sounds good. I'll meet you there?

Can't wait to see you, heart emoji

"Who ya texting?" Trent says, pulling me from my thoughts.

"No one," I say and he narrows his eyes at me.

"Jeremy?"

I did tell my best friends about Jeremy. I had to tell someone. They know dating is hard for me, and why, so it was a no brainer.

"Yeah."

"How's it going with him?"

"Fine, I guess."

"Fine? You guess? Sounds like a match made in heaven."

"I mean, I don't know. I like him. He's been really nice."

"But he's not Chris," Trent says. It's a statement not a question.

I swallow. I know better than to still be hoping or wishing for anything to happen between me and Chris, but it still hurts every time I have to remind myself that the reality is, he doesn't want me.

"I'll get over it," I say. "I will. And maybe Jeremy is the way to do that."

"Just don't do anything you don't want to do, huh?"

I nod, and decide it's time for another soda. I also decide that being twenty-one would be amazing right about now because I could really use some alcohol.

SEVEN

PARIS

When I get home it's almost two in the morning, and I'm wiped. I'm also surprised to see the light on in Chris's room. I was hoping he'd be fast asleep by now, and when I knock on his door there's no answer, even after I call his name.

Giving up, I turn the knob and push the door open slightly in case he's in there and just didn't hear me. Maybe he has headphones in or something. I keep pushing until I spot Chris at his desk.

His laptop is open, there's a barely touched bowl of pasta next to him, and two cans of RedBull. And he's asleep, his head resting on his desk, mouth slightly open and drooling onto his folded arms. His earbuds are still in his ears but there's no music playing as far as I can tell.

Fuck. It's killing me to see him like this. I move closer and pick up the cans of RedBull. Both empty. I take them and the barely touched pasta back to the kitchen. Then I return to his room and rest my hand gently on his shoulder, shaking him.

"Chris, wake up," I tell him. I shake him harder when he doesn't move a muscle. God if I couldn't hear his soft snoring I'd think he was dead. And that thought terrifies me.

"Chris, wake up," I repeat, louder this time and shake him more forcibly. "Hey, come on." I clap my hands really loud in front of his face and that makes him jerk. He snorts slightly and blinks, lifting his head. His skin is slightly ashen, his eyes are unfocused and bloodshot, and I want to fucking scream at him to take better care of himself.

"Pip?" he says softly, and my chest squeezes. "Hey, what's wrong?" He wipes the drool from his face and cringes. Then pulls the earbuds from his ears and sets them on his desk.

"I came home and you were asleep. Let's get you into bed." I grip his arm and try to help him stand.

He shakes his head. "No, fuck, I need to work on this paper." He rubs his eyes and blinks at the screen. "What the fuck? What is 'important in whoever that is for us' supposed to mean?"

I have no idea, but it's right there. The last line on the page. And is he seriously trying to write right now? When he can't even keep his eyes open and his brain is clearly not braining?

"Uh, no you don't. You need to sleep. Don't you have to be up at seven?"

He groans and lets me help him up. I hold his arm and pull him towards the bed. He collapses even as he mumbles about needing to change and brush his teeth, and I'm thinking both of those things can be skipped. I pull the blankets up over him and he's asleep once again before I even reach the door and turn out the light.

CHRIS

"Chris, can I talk to you for a second, please?" Amanda, my boss says. It's late afternoon and I've been up since the crack of dawn after only getting five hours of sleep. I was in classes this morning and headed to work straight after. I should have called out so I could get some more sleep. I'm exhausted and I know I've been messing up my last few orders and the customers here at *Spill the Beans* haven't been happy. But calling out means getting less money and every cent matters. Of course if I screw up so much I get fired that wouldn't help either.

My coworkers glance at me, pity in their expressions, mixed with mild annoyance. I sigh and make my way towards the door that leads to the break room, supply closet, and Amanda's small office.

I enter her office behind her and she closes the door. I don't even get the chance to sit before she turns to me, her green eyes stern, but mixed with compassion. "Go home, Chris." She's small, with pale skin and red hair, in her mid thirties, and she's a great boss. I hate letting her down.

"I'm fine," I tell her. "I'll do better. I'm sorry."

She holds her hand up. "I don't need you to be sorry, Chris. I need you to go home. You're running on empty. I can't in good conscience let you keep working. And your shift is over in forty five minutes anyway. I want you to rest. I've been worried about you."

For fuck's sake. Why is everyone so worried about me? How many times do I have to keep telling people I'm fine?

"I don't want you to come in again until Monday and I expect you to get some sleep. I know how much this job means to you, but it's not more important than your health and safety."

I grind my teeth. It pisses me off that people think they know how to handle my life better than I do, or that they think they know what's best for me.

"I know it doesn't feel like it," she says, "but I'm trying to help because I care about you. I've made you take breaks before. If you can't be okay with this I'll have to cut your hours back. It's just one shift, Chris. Use the time to catch up on some sleep, do some self care."

I almost scoff. Like I'm going to get in a bubble bath with wine and chocolate or something. I don't fucking need self-care. I need to work.

I have to keep myself from sneering the words out. "I guess I'll see you Monday, then." Then I turn and walk out.

As soon as I drop my keys in the basket by the front door my phone buzzes in my pocket. When I pull it out I see it's a FaceTime call from my sister, Janelle. And even though I'm still miffed at Amanda, I take a second to breathe, put on my "I'm great" face, and swipe.

"Hey, little sis," I greet with a smile. "How's it going?"

"Hey, butthead," she says with a grin. "I'm good. I miss you, though."

"Yeah, I miss you guys, too. I'm hoping to make it home for Christmas this year."

"God, that's forever far away," she pouts. "But I'll keep my fingers crossed."

"How's school?" I ask, making my way to my room and falling onto my bed.

"Good. Spanish class is my favorite."

Janelle has always been interested in learning other languages and she's been trying to teach herself Japanese since they don't have that option in middle school. She's been wanting to take Spanish for the last two years and the class always filled up before she could sign up, so I know how excited she is. I'm super impressed because learning a new language is hard, and I fucking suck at it.

"How's chorus? You guys have a concert coming up soon, right?"

She beams. "Yeah, we have a fall concert in October and another one right before Christmas. I even have a solo this year. I'm nervous, but super excited, too."

"Oh, wow, that's awesome. You'll have to make sure Mom and Dad take a video. I don't want to miss it."

She grins and there's a slight tinge of pink in her bronze colored cheeks.

"Who are you talking to?" I hear. "Your boyfriend?"

"No," she snaps. "It's Chris."

A second later my other sister, Ruby, pokes her face in the camera.

"Hi, big brother!" she chimes, waving at me. Her dark brown curls frame her face, and I smile at how all three of us look so much like our mom. We have some of Dad's features, too. Janelle has Dad's nose and so do I. And Ruby has his green eyes.

"Hey, munchkin. How's soccer going?"

"Ooh, so good, we're kicking butt this year!"

"It's literally been three weeks and you've had two games," Janelle retorts.

"And we've won both times," Ruby jibes back, then sticks her tongue out.

"You look tired," she says, turning her gaze back to the screen, and I have to keep from rolling my eyes.

"What's this about a boyfriend?" I ask, raising an eyebrow at Janelle. Ruby giggles and Janelle pokes her in the ribs.

"Nothing," Janelle says. "There's no boyfriend. She's just being annoying."

"Uh huh. Whoever he is, he's not good enough for you."

She rolls her eyes. "There's no boyfriend. I don't have time for boys. They're annoying."

"And dumb," Ruby pipes up.

"Hey," I say with a chuckle. "I'm a boy."

"Yeah, but you're different," Ruby assures me. "Most of the time."

I laugh again. "Thanks. How's Mom?"

"Mom is just fine," I hear, and then the phone is moving and it's Mom's face taking up my screen. She looks as exhausted as I feel but she gives me a huge smile and her brown eyes sparkle. Her warm brown skin is slightly ashen and it looks like she's lost weight since I saw her last, which makes my stomach churn, but she's up and moving around, which is a good sign.

"You two have chores to do, don't you?" she chides my sisters gently.

They mumble their complaints in unison and shout goodbye to me as they walk away.

"Hi Mom," I say.

"How's my baby boy?" She takes a seat on Janelle's bed while she talks to me. Her curly brown hair is up in a ponytail and she's wearing an oversized purple sweater. "I haven't heard from you in a while. You doing okay?"

"Yeah, of course."

"How's work? Not too much for you?"

"Nope, I'm good. Busy, but good."

"You sure? You don't need anything? You can't possibly be earning enough to pay for all your expenses working half time. The rent money we're sending is enough?"

"Yes, I promise, I don't need anything," I tell her. I'm also not going to correct her on how many hours I work because she wouldn't be okay with it. She and Dad barely let me get a job in the first place because they don't want me struggling to keep my grades up. The only way I could convince them was to "promise" to keep it part time and that I would stop if it was too much. I can't though. Not with everything they're dealing with. Not with everything she's dealing with. The last thing they need is to be worried about me. I hate that they're already paying the rent on my apartment, and I'm determined to make sure they don't have to pay for anything else. I'm taking care of food, books, car maintenance, gas. And whatever I'm not spending is going towards saving up for graduate school because I refuse to let them help with that. They have never talked directly with me about their finances, but I know things are tight, and ultimately I'm hoping I can save up enough to even help with some of the expenses. Like treatment for Mom or ballet classes for Ruby. Or even paying them back for all the rent money once I graduate. I know there are times where Mom goes without her PT, medication, or other visits because of finances. I'd refuse the rent money if I thought I could get away with it, but then they'd know I was working far more hours than we agreed on. I'd suggested staying at home and working full time before I started college and all that had gotten me was a stern talking to and two fierce glares, as well as Dad telling me there was "no way in hell" I was giving up a full ride scholarship and a chance at my dream job because of them. They also keep reminding me that once I'm actually a PT, I can help Mom with some of her treatment. God, if I ever get there that is. It feels like a lifetime away.

"Have you been able to work at all lately?" I ask. Mom is one of the most talented artists there is, and maybe I'm a little biased about that, but her work is incredible. Her focus is landscapes, but she also does portraits and animals. Unfortunately, ever since she got sick her ability to do any art has been severely diminished, and because her health is so poor, she's unable to take on clients with specific requests because she can't guarantee being able to meet a deadline, or even finish the project at all. Instead she's sticking to things that she decides to paint for herself with whatever minimal energy or time she has. That also means that she's not making nearly as much as she used to with her work.

I hate it, because it's so much of who she is and it makes her so happy to create things and share them with the world. I just want her to be able to do what she loves again without it causing her pain or making her sick, but I don't think that will ever happen.

"Sometimes," she tells me. "A lot of times it helps to create. It can be a distraction and an outlet. But it depends on the day. I'm not giving up, though. It's gonna take a lot more than these stupid illnesses to get me to stop creating." She grins. Mom's a fighter. She always has been. Both of my parents are amazing and I admire them so much. They deserve better than what this life has thrown at them.

"How's Dad?"

"He's good, baby. We're both good. Don't you worry about us, okay? He's keeping busy at work, and you know how he fusses over me, but I'm fine. I don't always feel so great, but I have an amazing husband and three incredible children that I'm so proud of. We both are."

"Yeah, thanks, Mom." I barely get the words out. Partly because I'm trying to hold in the emotions clawing at my chest, and partly because I'm fucking exhausted. It's not fair that she has to deal with all of this. It's not fair to any of us, but least of all, her.

"It sounds like you need some rest, baby. I should let you go. I'll talk to you soon, okay? Please don't hesitate to tell us if you need anything. We love you."

"Love you, too, Mom. Say hi to Dad for me."

"I will, sweetie. Bye."

"Bye."

I end the call, and roll onto my side. I quickly wipe away the tears that slide down my cheeks, and before I know it, I'm fast asleep.

When I wake it's to the smell of something delicious coming from the kitchen.

I groan and roll out of bed, feeling semi human, and stumble my way down the hall and into the kitchen.

I can't help the grin that splits my face when I see Paris shimmying to the beat of whatever music must be playing in his headphones as he stirs something in a pot on the stove. His head bops back and forth as his hips sway and the skirt he's wearing swishes back and forth. He's wearing pink fish net tights but no shoes and his feet twist and slide on the hard floor as he moves.

God I miss him, and the realization is so strong there's a pang in my chest. I make my way over to him and tap his shoulder. He nearly jumps out of his skin and lets out a shriek that has me trying to hold back my laughter as he spins around with the spatula he was holding in his hand like he's ready to beat me with it, eyes wide. He takes his airpods out of his ears and gasps, "Jesus Christ you butthead, I thought you were an intruder or something. You scared the stuffing out of me."

I do laugh now. "And you were going to defend yourself with a spatula?"

He glares. "Hey, I'm lethal, okay? Don't you shit on my spatula." He waves it at me and I laugh again, even as the sauce from it drips on the floor and splatters over my face and shirt, as well as the nearby cupboards.

"Oh, fuck, sorry," he gasps, as he sets the spatula down and hurries to grab a washcloth. I take it from him and start to wipe up the mess, starting with myself.

"No, I'm sorry. You're kinda cute when you're all riled up, though."

He blushes and I tell myself that I have to stop opening my mouth around him and saying shit like that.

"I didn't expect you to be home," he says as he works on what looks like fajitas. My stomach growls and it's not subtle. He laughs.

"Hungry?"

"Starving," I admit.

"Well, it will be finished soon. Why don't you get out plates?"

I do, and set them on the counter. I also fill two glasses with water. When the food is ready Paris plates it and we bring it to the table. The table with the pretty flowers in the center and the artwork hanging on the adjacent wall and the pink and white seat cushions, which honestly are way more comfortable than sitting on a hard chair.

It's taken some getting used to but I really enjoy the touches he's added to the place now, mostly I think because they remind me of him. The pink couch is taking a little bit longer than everything else, but I'll get there, I'm sure. It's not like I'm home all that often anyway.

"Wow, this is amazing," I mumble through a mouthful of fajita.

"Thank you," he beams. "I enjoy cooking."

"I enjoy eating, so it works out great." I wink at him and he chuckles.

"You wanna hang out tonight?" I ask. I honestly should be doing homework, but I never see him, and being around him makes me feel better.

For some reason, he blushes. "I can't. I have plans."

Oh. Of course he has plans. He's Paris, and it's not like he had any reason to suspect I'd want to hang out with him since we never do. Still though, I can't help but be disappointed. "An LGBTQ club thing?"

He shakes his head.

"Hanging out with Trent and Vanessa?"

Another head shake and his cheeks are even more pink than before, the blush reaching his ears now. "Oh," I say out loud, realization dawning on me. "Are you, I mean . . ." god I don't really want to finish that sentence because I hate the idea of Paris hooking up with someone. It makes me sick to my stomach. Why does it make me sick to my stomach?

"No," he says, shaking his head. "It's not a hookup. It's a date. With a guy. Well, obviously a guy. His name is Jeremy, and he's really great. We're seeing the movie they're showing on campus." He bites his lip and I'm pretty sure it's to keep himself from talking some more.

How did I not know he was seeing someone? I mean, at least it's not a random hookup, but my stomach isn't feeling any less queasy at the idea of him being on a date. In fact, I find I'm really not hungry anymore. And I have no idea why. It's none of my concern who he goes out with. Why do I care?

"How long have you been seeing each other?" I ask.

"Not long. It's pretty new."

"But you like him?" Why the fuck am I treating him like this is an interrogation? He's allowed to date and fuck whoever he wants and it's none of my goddamn business.

"Yeah, I think so. He's nice."

I force the words out but they feel like ash on my tongue. "Have a good time." I decide that since I no longer feel like eating, and Paris has plans, I might as well get some home-work done after all.

I sit at my desk, pop my earbuds in and turn on Tracy Chapman. I'm so used to having her songs in my head when I study that I have a hard time studying without them. There's something about them that helps me relax and focus. Usually. Tonight though, I find myself distracted.

Distracted wondering what Paris is doing on his date, wondering if Jeremy is treating him right, if Paris is letting Jeremy kiss him, if he's going back to Jeremy's place and letting Jeremy fuck him, or if Jeremy is making him blush, or if Jeremy gets to see those sexy as hell panties on him, or if Jeremy's heart feels three sizes too big when Paris smiles at him.

EIGHT

PARIS

"Hey, you okay?" Jeremy asks as we get settled on the blanket he brought. There's dozens of other students in front of the outdoor screen they have set up on the quad and it smells like popcorn, which is making my mouth water. But I can't stop thinking about Chris.

"Yeah, of course," I lie. Dinner was going great until I mentioned my date, and then he got really weird. I know better than to think he's jealous, but he seemed bothered for some reason that I can't figure out.

"You wanna talk about it?"

"Nah, it's fine."

"Well, maybe this will help." He hands me a bag of M&Ms and I grin.

"My favorite. Thank you."

"You want popcorn now or later?"

"Is both an option?"

He laughs. "Be right back."

When he returns I'm sitting on the blanket, my oversized sweater wrapped around me. I'm wearing fleece lined leggings since it's a little chilly, and I've got my black UGG boots on. He hands me a bag of popcorn and then reaches behind him and grabs a blanket, tucking it over my shoulders as I shiver. Then his arm comes around me.

A second later his lips brush my ear when he says, "You look really cute tonight, by the way."

"Thank you," I say with a blush.

"Can I kiss you again?"

I turn to him and nod. His lips brush against mine softly, and I kiss him back, telling myself this is what I need to move on from Chris, the boy who will never love me back, never want me, never see me as anything but a friend.

And something inside me aches.

CHRIS

It's Monday afternoon at *Spill the Beans* and I've been on shift for a couple of hours, breathing in the scent of roasted beans and baked goods that always make my stomach grumble, when the bell above the door chimes and I look up from the register to see Paris sauntering in, holding hands with a tall, attractive guy with dark hair and a slender physique. Jeremy, no doubt.

My chest tightens as emotions roll through me that I can't quite parse out. I try not to examine that too much because I'm afraid of where it might lead. Instead I do my best to smile at them, and not look at their clasped hands as they approach the counter.

Paris's eyes are wide when he sees me and then a huge smile breaks out over his perfect face. "Oh my god, I didn't know this is where you worked," he says, bouncing up and down on the balls of his feet. "I mean, it makes sense, right, there's only so many coffee shops around campus. This is so cool, now you can meet Jeremy." He turns to his . . . boyfriend. What kind of a name is Jeremy, anyway?

"Jeremy, this is Chris, my roommate." As exuberant as

Paris is he seems a little flustered, maybe even nervous? So I do my best to not be a dick.

"Hey," Jeremy says, holding out his hand. "Nice to meet you."

"You too." Don't tell me I'm not a good actor because that was the finest bit of lying I ever did. "What can I get you guys?" Whatever I get for Jeremy I'll be spitting in it. Okay, not really, but I'm sorely tempted.

"Oh, right, um . . . " Paris scans the menu biting his lip, and my fists clench under the counter when Jeremy rests his hand on the small of his back and presses a kiss to his blond waves. I have to keep from clenching my jaw when he looks back at me and force a smile instead.

"I'll take a medium pumpkin spice latte," Paris says.

"Hot or cold?"

"Definitely hot."

I look at Jeremy who still has his hand on Paris's back. "I'll do the toasted marshmallow mocha. Medium and hot."

I ring them up and take Jeremy's card, then get to work while they find a table. It's fairly slow right now so the only people in here besides them are a single female college age student buried in homework, and two women in their thirties sitting together and chatting.

Jeremy and Paris find a two person table by a window that's been decorated in fall window clings. Jeremy slides Paris's chair out for him and I scowl.

I decide I hate him. I don't know him at all. He's probably not a terrible person if Paris is dating him, and he's pulling out chairs for his date, but I hate him nonetheless. I hate him even more when Paris blushes, and a little more still when I hear Paris laugh as I'm making their drinks; not like a chuckle, but like a full body belly laugh that carries through the entire cafe and has him apologizing seconds later when the other patron's heads pop up, and then laughing some more.

I consider once more spitting in Jeremy's latte. And I have

to force myself not to stare at them like a total creeper while they talk and laugh and do that looking into each other's eyes thing couples do. Gross.

What the hell is wrong with me? I should be happy for him. He's getting out there, meeting people, having fun. Moving on from the kiss, which is what I fucking want. So why is this Jeremy guy setting me off? I don't know, but something about him just doesn't sit right with me.

And why can't I stop wishing that the person sitting across from Paris right now was me?

NINE

PARIS

After spending the morning hiking with Trent, and the afternoon shopping with Vanessa, I'm finally back at home. It's early October now and it's getting colder out, especially in the evenings. And even though it's not quite evening I'm ready to be comfortable and cozy, so I change out of my skirt and tights and into my unicorn onesie before plopping myself down at the kitchen table with my laptop to work on the homework for my *Introduction to Psychology* course.

In a couple of hours I'm planning to make dinner and then heading out again for karaoke night with the LGBTQ club.

An hour and forty five minutes later I decide my twink brain is fried, and it's time for a break from staring at my screen, so I close my laptop and head for the kitchen. On the menu tonight is parmesan chicken and I'm in the process of shoving the chicken in the oven when the front door opens and Chris walks in.

"Hey, perfect timing," I say. "Dinner will be ready in about half an hour."

He smiles at me as he slides off his shoes and then drags

himself to his bedroom. "I'm gonna lay down until it's ready."

I nod, and then hear the door click behind him.

When the oven beeps, letting me know dinner is ready I take it out, throw some microwaveable mixed veggies in the, well, microwave, and then go down the hall towards Chris's room. I knock, and when there's no answer I open the door. He's passed out on his bed, face down, his shoes and jacket still on, snoring softly, and I decide not to wake him. I also decide that I want to be here when he wakes up. Having your life revolve around classes and work must be lonely, and I don't want him to feel alone right now.

I eat my dinner in front of the television, watching an episode of *Queer Eye* (they always make me cry), and then decide to do some work on the essay for the *General Biology* class I'm in this semester.

Not surprisingly, I get a text from Trinity asking where I am.

Not gonna make it tonight, I tell her. *Everything's fine. I just decided to stay at home.*

Okay, she replies. *See you next time.*

It's two hours later when Chris stumbles out of his room, and when he does he looks surprised to see me.

"Hey," I say. "Dinner's in the fridge."

"Thanks," he mumbles as I close my laptop.

"You okay?" I know it's a touchy subject, and honestly useless because even if he's not okay he'll tell me he is.

"Yeah, of course."

"Do you want to watch something with me while you eat?"

He blinks. "You don't have plans?"

I shake my head.

"Yeah, sure," he agrees, grabbing his food out of the microwave. He joins me on the couch and gives a small chuckle. "Nice jammies."

"Thank you," I say, smiling.

"They look comfy," he adds as he shoves food in his mouth.

"They are. Feel them, they're super soft." He blinks at me, but then reaches his hand over and rubs my shoulder. Jesus, just that touch has my body lighting up like nobody's business. Why the hell is it like that with him? I don't know, but I've been on multiple dates with Jeremy and his touch never makes me feel like that. Being near him, sharing space with him, talking to him, doesn't make me want to rip my clothes off and crawl in his lap.

Fuck, I'm really sucking at moving on from Chris.

"Wow, that is soft," he murmurs, and then his eyes meet mine, and for a second I think I see something there. Something that I've never seen before, but it's gone in an instant when he turns his gaze away from mine.

"What are we watching?" he asks.

"I watched an episode of *Queer Eye* earlier, we can do another one."

"Sure."

"Warning, I'm a cryer," I tell him.

He sets his plate down and goes down the hall towards his room. For a second I think he literally just left me there because he doesn't want to deal with my emotions, but then he's returning, sitting even closer to me than he was before, which I'm not complaining about, by the way, and hands me a box of tissues.

"Just in case," he says with a grin. It's tired, but it's so beautiful it makes my heart flutter.

Halfway through the show I'm bawling, dabbing my eyes with the tissues and he's got his arm around my shoulders, my head resting on his shoulder.

"You okay?" he asks, and I feel his fingers running through my hair. A shiver races down my spine and my dick jerks. Fuck. This is so not fair.

"Yeah," I say. I sniffle and lift my head even though every single part of me wants to stay right where I am. But I can't if

I'm supposed to be getting over him. God, he smells so good too, just his body wash and a tinge of sweat, but fuck, it makes my toes curl, and I never feel safer than when his arm is around me.

After the show is over I expect him to tell me he needs to get some homework done, but instead he asks, "You wanna play *Mario Kart*?"

"You wanna play *Mario Kart* with me?" I don't know why I'm so stunned, and I must be making an epic face because he laughs.

"Yeah, why not?"

"Um, well, I think I've played like three times in all my life and that was only because Phoenix and Preston made me, and I sucked at it. Like, I couldn't stay on the track to save my life and kept getting turned around to the point where everyone was lapping me multiple times. And I'm pretty sure the bananas have a vendetta against me even though I don't know what I ever did to them. If you think you're ready for that level of magnificence, though, sure I'll take you on."

He laughs again, fuller and deeper, and it warms my insides. And hey, if me sucking at *Mario Kart* brings that sparkle to his eyes, I'll happily be terrible at it.

"They have changed some things since you played. You can choose to set it up so you can't fall off the track at least. Not sure there's much help for getting turned around. We can get rid of the bananas if you want. You can pick which items you want to include."

"Oh, well, no we should definitely have the bananas cause that's part of the fun, but I'm completely willing to get rid of the inky squid thing that takes up the entire screen and makes it impossible to drive."

He gets the game set up, since I have no idea about such things. I think it's been at least three years since I touched any kind of gaming controller. He helps me figure out the contraption and when the screen with the character options shows up I choose Yoshi, and of course I make him pink.

Then I go through the grueling process of selecting a vehicle and a parachute. So many options!

Chris gives me pointers on what vehicles and parachutes are the best, and I decide to take a chance and not use the Smart Steering option.

Adventure awaits.

He lets me pick the first track, which holy bejesus there's way more of them than is called for. But I finally settle on *Squeaky Clean Sprint* which looks like it takes place in a bathroom. I'm already laughing when we start.

"Oh my god, this is hilarious," I comment as we drive, but I'm honestly cracking up so much I'm already in last place after the first ten seconds.

Chris is laughing, too, but I'm pretty sure it's at my antics, especially since I'm up off the couch, shrieking and squealing and exclaiming "Oh my god," "fuck", "shit," and "No, no, no", practically jumping up and down as I try desperately to keep pink Yoshi on track.

Spoiler alert, it's not working, but I'm okay with that because Chris is laughing hysterically next to me now.

When we finally make it across the finish line I'm in twelfth place, go figure, and Chris managed to skate by in fourth, though I'm guessing he usually does better than that.

"Sorry I distracted you," I say, even though he doesn't seem upset.

He shakes his head. "You make me so damn happy, Pip," he says, ruffling my hair, and god I don't know what to say to that.

CHRIS

A week later I'm working on some research for my Senior Seminar class when I get a text from Preston. I haven't hung out with him in weeks and it sucks. I mean, he's come into *Spill the Beans* a few times, either alone or with Jackson, and I honestly think he's doing it more so he can see me and less so he can get his caffeine fix, which is honestly really sweet. I miss him, though. I miss having a social life in general. I just keep telling myself the payout will be worth it, and I hope I'm right. I do need to find time to hang out with him, though, even if it's only for an hour.

Hey, come hang out at Rave tonight with me and Jackson? Parker and Rory are coming, too.

I'm beat, and I should be focusing on my school work and not going out with friends, but god I need it. And maybe it will be the perfect way to get my mind off a certain perky twink who seems to have invaded my thoughts lately.

What time? I type back.

8?

I'll see you then.

Yes!

I grin.

It's only a few minutes after eight when I make my way into the rowdy club. There's dozens of sweaty bodies on the dance floor, a packed bar, and upbeat music playing. It smells like sweat, alcohol, and disinfectant. The air is charged and I realize how much I miss doing things like this.

I spot the gang at the bar. Parker is so big he's hard to miss even in the crowd. He's sitting on a bar stool, Rory standing between his splayed thighs and they're grinning like idiots and giving each other little bird-like pecks on the lips. It's disgusting. And adorable. Rory's engagement ring catches the light and sparkles as I make my way over.

Preston is standing with his back to the bar, and in front of him is Jackson, their hands on each other's hips, both smiling and laughing. And I have the sudden realization that I'm not experiencing all the hurt, anger, and confusion I used to when it came to seeing them together.

As soon as Preston sees me a huge smile splits his face. "Hey, you made it." He claps me on the shoulder as I join him and order a beer. Jackson subtly steps away, moving closer to

Rory and Parker, and letting me have Preston to myself, which I appreciate.

"I did. Thanks for inviting me."

"Of course, man, I miss you."

I don't think he means to make me feel guilty, but I do. "Sorry, I know I've been busy."

"Hey, it's okay," he assures me.

"Hey Chris!" Parker pipes up. "How's it going?" He holds his hand out in a closed fist and I bump it with mine.

"Hey, guys, you seem happy," I say, ignoring the question. "Make any wedding plans yet?"

Rory blushes fiercely and Parker grins like a lunatic. "Not really," Rory says, pushing his glasses up on his nose even though they haven't moved. "We're waiting until after graduation so things calm down a bit first."

"Why don't we find a table?" Jackson suggests, then leads the rest of the group through the crowd to a free booth in the corner. We slide in, Rory letting out a squeak when Parker pulls him onto his lap, but he grins and nuzzles his fiance's neck.

"You guys are gross," Jackson says and Rory sticks his tongue out at his best friend. Jackson chuckles and takes a sip of his drink.

"How's play practice going?" I ask, and Preston beams while Jackson looks as stoic as ever.

"It's good," Jackson says. "Sucking the life out of me but I love it."

"They're doing *West Side Story*," Preston says with a wide smile. "And Jackson is playing Tony."

"Nice," I say. "Can't wait to see it."

"Oh, that reminds me, I got tickets for you and Paris," Preston says. "November 13, 7 pm. You guys can meet me in the lobby of the theater."

"We're coming too!" Rory cheers. "My bestie is amazing!"

We all chuckle as Parker murmurs, "I think he's getting drunk."

"You guys wanna dance, give these two some time to catch up?" Jackson says to Rory and Parker, and they nod, scooting out of the booth.

We talk, filling each other in on classes that we're not in together, complaining about homework assignments and frustrating professors. We update each other on our families, and thankfully he avoids the topic of how much I'm working, because I don't want to get into it with him tonight.

We have a couple of beers, we laugh and tease each other, and it feels really good to be here, spending this time with him.

Then, for some reason, I find myself looking towards the front door, and a sick feeling settles in the pit of my stomach when I see Paris and Jeremy, once again holding hands and making their way to the dance floor.

My chest tightens and I have to force myself not to stare at them as Jeremy grips Paris's hips and they start to move.

"You okay?" Preston asks, looking out into the bar where my gaze is fixed on his brother and his brother's boyfriend.

"Yeah."

"Hey, that must be Jeremy," he says. "You met him?"

I nod, then take a sip of my drink. "He's okay."

"Paris seems to like him a lot."

I grunt and try to avoid clenching my fists under the table as Jeremy pulls Paris closer.

"You wanna get out there and dance?" Preston asks, oblivious to my inner turmoil.

"Nah, but you go ahead," I say.

"You sure?"

I nod, and he goes to join his boyfriend. I get up and make my way through the crowd, suddenly desperate for another drink.

As I sip on my third beer of the night my gaze locks on Paris and Jeremy again. Yes, I'm fully aware I am staring at them like a mega creeper, but I can't stop. Jeremy's hands move from Paris's low back to his ass, and I find myself gripping my beer bottle even tighter, my jaw clenching. When Jeremy squeezes Paris's ass and then kisses him like Paris is his life's breath, that's when I decide I've had enough.

But before I can leave, something catches my gaze and I look over to see Jackson's eyes locked on me. They flit from me to Paris and Jeremy even as he moves with Preston, who's back is to me.

I turn away, my heart slamming in my chest and my hands damp with sweat and the perspiration from the beer bottle. I set the bottle on the bar, grab my jacket from the coat room, and head for the door.

So much for getting my mind off of Paris tonight.

TEN

PARIS

"Fuck, you taste good," Jeremy murmurs as his lips brush against mine, his tongue dipping inside for another taste. His hand works its way from my shoulder, down to my hip as he kisses me, then slides along my thigh and then under my skirt.

I jerk back when his hand comes in contact with my cock.

His hand leaves, but his expression is pained when I meet his gaze. "Paris?"

I shake my head.

He sighs. "You're still not ready?"

I shake my head again, my skin feeling hot all over and my face flaming. Tears sting at the corners of my eyes.

"Is it me?" he asks.

"I don't think so," I tell him, my voice quiet.

"Then what is it? Are you ace or something?"

The way he says it isn't accusatory, just like he wants to understand.

"I don't think so. I mean, I like the idea of sex, I want it, I just need to feel connected to the person first." *And there's only*

He frowns, his eyes sad. "We've been dating for a month, and all we've done is kiss. I like it, I like you, Paris, a lot, but I need more than that. Maybe that makes me selfish, but I do. I want sex, and I'm not trying to make you feel bad or pressure you, I just . . . " he sighs, and I know what's coming. "I think we should stop seeing each other. Yeah? I can't keep hoping that you'll want me that way. When we first met and you said you didn't do one night stands I thought it might be a couple of weeks, at most, and I guess I'm not as patient as I thought I was. I'm sorry about that."

Tears are sliding down my cheeks now because I knew this would happen, and I feel for the millionth time like there's something wrong with me. I feel guilty, like I led him on, made him waste his time on me, but I didn't mean to. I honestly thought I could want sex with him eventually. Maybe I could, but I need more time. Time he doesn't want to give me.

"Hey, it's not your fault," he says, wiping the tears from my cheeks. "Please don't feel bad. I'm sorry I'm such a horn dog."

I chuckle slightly as fresh tears fall and I hug my pink heart shaped pillow to my chest. "You don't have to be sorry."

"Neither do you," he says, squeezing my hand. "I want you to be happy, Paris. I hope you find the guy who sets your heart on fire. Someone who adores you, and appreciates you, and who you can have some seriously hot sex with." He grins at me and I manage another chuckle, my cheeks flushing.

"I'd really like to still be friends," he says. "Like, actual friends, not pretend friends who say they are but don't ever talk to each other."

"Yeah, okay," I agree, "I'd like that."

He gives a soft smile. "Good." Then he leans in to kiss my

wet cheek. "Take care of yourself, beautiful," he murmurs, and then he's gone.

CHRIS

When I get home that night it's late, thanks to the group project I had after work and classes, and I'm beyond beat. I grab my wallet off the dash and slide it into my pants pocket before I head inside, feeling like I could fall asleep on my feet.

But my exhaustion takes a back seat when I see Paris curled up on the sofa in his koala bear onesie, hugging a pillow, tears sliding down his cheeks. My heart aches at the sight and all my senses go on alert as I drop my bag and keys and hurry over to him.

"Hey, Pip, what's wrong?" I ask, putting my arm over his shoulders as he wipes tears away.

"Nothing," he says, but then cries harder as he leans into me, his head resting on my shoulder.

"Oh, come on, you don't expect me to believe that, do you?" I rub his arm and he sniffles.

It takes him a moment, but eventually he says, "Jeremy and I broke up."

Oh. Fuck. I'll admit I wasn't Jeremy's biggest fan, at least not when it came to seeing him with Paris, but I hate this. I hate that Paris is upset and hurting.

Before I can say anything though, he adds, "He wanted sex and I wasn't ready. Just like my last boyfriend."

Oh.

"Sometimes I think there's something wrong with me," he blubbers. "That I haven't had sex yet and I'm nineteen."

"Hey, look at me," I tell him gently, still processing the fact that he's a virgin. I really didn't expect that. He lifts his head, his eyes still watery, and the tear tracks on his cheeks are enough to gut me. "There's nothing wrong with you, okay? You don't owe anyone anything, least of all your body. And you should never do something you don't feel comfortable with or aren't ready for."

He nods, and wipes his nose on the sleeve of his pajamas. "I mean, I get that sex is supposed to be amazing, and that it's a big deal to a lot of people, and lots of people are fine with casual sex and sleeping together after not knowing each other very well, or at all, but I've never been like that. I thought if I dated someone long enough maybe I would feel that way, want to be close to them but so far . . ." he trails off and more tears fall. "At least Jeremy was nicer about it. My last boyfriend texted me to break up after I told him I wasn't ready for sex and we'd been together for three weeks. He'd been pressuring me the entire time. All his text said was 'it's not working out'."

I scowl. "Well, he's an asshole."

Paris gives a slight chuckle. His head comes back to rest on my shoulder, his legs curled up on the sofa. I run my fingers through his hair and he sighs. "I just want it to mean something, you know? The first time? I want someone who'll treat me like a princess. Make me feel special. I mean, honestly being treated like a princess is kinda my life's dream in general."

I chuckle this time, but truthfully I want that for him, too. He deserves it. He deserves to be spoiled and pampered and doted on. "Hey, you know what always makes things better, especially break-ups?"

He lifts his head, wiping tears away. "What?"

"Ice cream. Wanna go get some? My treat."

"Oh, you don't have to do that."

"I want to. That's what friends do, right?"

He gives a soft smile. "Yeah." Then he looks down at himself. "I'm not exactly dressed to go out."

I shrug. "I don't mind."

He looks scandalized. "If you think I'm going out in public like this you're nuts."

I laugh. "Change then. I'll wait."

He scurries off, and I'll be honest I kind of miss the onesie because he looks so adorable and cozy in them, but when he returns he looks just as good, dressed more casually than usual in leggings and an oversized pink sweater that nearly reaches his knees. His hair is a bit tousled, which I love, and he's cleaned his face up, but didn't apply any new makeup.

"Ready?" I ask, and he nods. We slide our shoes on, grab our jackets, and make our way to the car.

Fortunately since we're in a college town there's a handful of ice cream places open late.

We drive to one that's just a few minutes from campus, and head inside. There's a sweet mixture of sugar, vanilla, chocolate, and banana in the air when we enter, and chatter coming from the small tables where friends and couples sit enjoying their treats.

We stand in line and peruse the menu. When we get to the counter Paris orders The Rainbow, which is cookie dough ice cream with extra cookie dough chunks, rainbow sprinkles and brownie bits. I get butter pecan and we take our orders to an empty table.

"Thanks for doing this," Paris says as he uses his spoon to play with his ice cream. "It's really nice of you."

"Of course. So, tell me why you decided to be a psychology major."

He blows out a breath. "Wow, that's kind of a big question actually." He takes a bite of his dessert and a little bit lands on his bottom lip when he pulls the spoon away. I find myself resisting the urge to reach over and swipe it off, and then his tongue darts out and my breath hitches. Jesus.

"You don't have to–" I start, but he shakes his head.

"I don't mind sharing. Especially with you. You've always made me feel safe, you know?" He gives me that sweet Paris smile and I practically melt right along with the ice cream. Fuck.

"The short story is that I had, or have, actually, a really great therapist myself. I mean, I think you know that I was seeing someone after we lost Phoenix." I nod. Preston's told me a lot about his older brother and what it was like for him when he passed, how hard it was on him, on everyone. But I never really knew Paris's side of things. "Well, I was seeing the same therapist before that, too, which honestly helped a lot, already having someone who I knew I could talk to if I needed it. And I did.

"I started seeing her when I was eleven, actually." He takes another bite and swallows. "It might surprise you to know this but I wasn't like all the other boys growing up. Or like my brothers." He grins, his tone light and teasing, his eyes filled with a mixture of emotions I can't quite parse out; a bit of pain, but also resilience, determination, a boatload of courage, and joy. I'm sure he hasn't had it easy growing up in our fucked up society and being who he is, which is something I can relate to, but he's made it this far and not apologized, and I admire that so damn much. I can't imagine him shrinking himself to fit others' ideals of who he should be, because who he is is absolutely beautiful inside and out.

"How so?" I ask, though I'm pretty sure I can guess what he means, but I want more. I want to know him. I want all he'll give me. He eyes me, but chuckles.

"Oh you know, I just had so much testosterone it was scary." I laugh and he laughs with me. "Let's just say I've always wanted to be a princess. Pretty dresses, make-up, nails, shoes, all of it. I wanted to be a princess all day every day as a toddler, even dressed up like princesses for Halloween for a few years, until I started to realize that I was getting judged for it. Realizing the other boys were "normal" and I wasn't. That I was "supposed to" be into sports and want to wrestle, and play video games and like girls. I mean, it didn't take long before I realized that the things I loved and enjoyed and made me feel so alive weren't things that were accepted by a lot of people, and as I got older that spark I had, started to dissipate, I guess? Even with all the support of my family. I mean, Phoenix and Preston even dressed up as fairies with me one Halloween so I wouldn't be alone. And they were a lot older, so imagine the teasing they went through because they loved me that much. But all the outside noise really got to me anyway. My parents tried to encourage me not to be someone I wasn't, but I was scared and hurt, and confused, you know? I wanted to fit in, to be liked. And I ended up really being someone I wasn't for all of my formative years, like all the way through elementary school."

A small smile creases his lips and he continues. "Phoenix was the one who really encouraged me to be myself over and over again. Said if people were bothered by it they weren't my people. I'd been seeing a therapist since the end of fourth grade because I was really nervous about middle school, and struggling a lot with my identity. I'd had a few breakdowns because I hated existing as a version of myself I didn't recognize. My parents wanted to help and support me, but they didn't really know how to. Talking to someone who specialized in LGBTQ issues was what gave me the courage to finally be me. That and meeting Trent and Vanessa, and having my family by my side. Preston had his head a little more in the clouds at the time," he chuckles, "but Phoenix was my biggest cheerleader. When I finally decided to dress how I wanted and start wearing make-up, he told me so many times how proud he was of me and how brave I was." Tears fill his eyes and start to slide down his cheeks. "He told me that even though I was the little brother he looked up to me."

Fuck. I wipe a tear from my own eye before reaching over to squeeze his hand. "I wish I could have met him. He sounds like a really cool guy."

Paris sniffles and nods. "He was. After he died I went through a period where I reverted to my old self, stopped being the real me again. I don't know if it was grief or rebellion or anger or what, but my counselor was really instrumental in helping me work through it and I got myself back. I just kept thinking about how Phoenix would have wanted me to be true to myself no matter what. It's taken a long time and a lot of struggle to get where I am, but I like myself. I'm proud of me and I can honestly say I don't care what anyone else thinks because when I put on my make-up or my jewelry or my pretty skirts I see my big brother smiling at me and telling me how proud he is."

"You're making me cry, Pip," I confess, though the evidence is on my face. I wipe away another tear and scoot closer, putting my arm around him and pulling him close, not caring that we're in public and everyone in this place can see us.

He sniffles and wipes his eyes. "All that to say," he says, a bit more casually, no doubt trying to lighten the mood. "I want to be a therapist and specialize in helping people in the LGBTQ community because it mattered to me so much, talking to someone who understood and knowing I wasn't alone when I was at my lowest. But also just because I think therapists in general are pretty fucking amazing. I don't know what I would have done if I hadn't had my therapist when Phoenix died or my parents got sick. I just want to help, you know?"

I nod and press a kiss to his hair. "You're gonna be amazing at it."

We sit in silence for a bit and I find myself wanting to share with him, things I've never told anyone but Preston. Things that are hard for me to talk about. But like he said earlier, with him, I feel safe. And it's hard to keep everything inside. Sometimes I feel like I'm going to explode, or like I just need to go out to the woods somewhere and fucking scream.

"My mom is sick," I murmur, and just the ability to get that off my chest and out in the air where it can breathe makes me feel a thousand pounds lighter.

He lifts his head. "Like cancer?"

I shake my head. "No, she uh . . . she has several different chronic illnesses."

"Oh. I don't know much about that."

I sigh. "Neither did I until it happened to her."

"How long?"

"Eight years."

"Oh, shit."

"She started feeling sick shortly after Ruby was born. Nausea, dizziness, light-headedness, extreme fatigue, migraines, fainting, digestive issues, debilitating chronic pain. She was super sensitive to noise all of a sudden, lots of brain fog. Just about everything in the book, and more symptoms kept popping up every month, it seemed. Took a couple of years of not knowing or understanding what was happening and seeing loads of different doctors until she finally got diagnosed with POTS and fibromyalgia."

"I've never heard of POTS. I have heard of fibromyalgia, though. That sounds really hard. For her and you guys."

"Yeah. I was fourteen when everything started and it freaked me out, honestly. My mom went from being this lively, vivacious person to someone who could only be out of bed a few hours a day and never for more than ten or fifteen minutes at a time. Janelle was six, and Dad was working full time and Ruby was a toddler. It was a lot. It still is. I mean, we've adapted as much as we can but . . . fuck." I rub my hand over my short curls, letting out another breath.

Now it's his turn to take my hand and squeeze, and it's amazing how much it helps. How much it grounds me.

"It fucking sucks," I admit. "One of the worst parts is that Mom was just starting to make a name for herself in the art community. She's incredible, honestly. Her online following was growing, she'd done lots of fairs and festivals, had her work in some local restaurants, even did showings at a few galleries and was featured in magazines. She made a lot of her money from doing commissions for people, too, but after she got sick she couldn't work nearly as much and things dwindled pretty fast. Even with things like Etsy and having her work on social media, it still sells, but she can't produce a lot of new art because she feels so sick all the time, which means our family has been surviving on one income and whatever random sales Mom's work happens to bring in that month, and with the cost of her medical treatment, it's nuts. I mean, ninety percent of the time if she is out of bed it's because she has another doctor's appointment of some kind. And my dad works his butt off, but I don't know how they're still staying afloat with everything."

"That's why you work so hard," he says. "You want to help, you don't want to be an extra burden."

I nod. "I know it's hard on Dad. He's exhausted. He's working all the time and taking care of Janelle and Ruby, and Mom, now, too. And it's been years. And everything is so damn expensive. Medications, supplements, lab work, chiropractic care, PT. She has a lot of different people she sees to try and manage her symptoms and some of it isn't covered by insurance, and even when it is it's super expensive, so I know they are overwhelmed. Plus, new symptoms keep popping up every time one seems to be settling a little. She's been in the hospital so much we're just used to it now." Now that I've started talking about all of this I can't stop.

"It's tough for my sisters, too. They were both so young when Mom got sick, and they haven't really known anything else. But no one understands if they say their mom can't attend a school function or a birthday party because she's sick, and she's still sick days or weeks or months later. She looks fine on the outside, you know, and so everyone assumes she is fine. That she's healthy.

"Sometimes I'm honestly not sure if being older when it happened and remembering how she used to be is better or worse. I hate that she's suffering and there's nothing I can do."

"I get that part," Paris says softly, giving my hand another squeeze. "It's not exactly the same. I wasn't watching my parents suffer for years. That must be awful. But when they had cancer I felt the exact same way. It was miserable, and terrifying."

"Sometimes I feel like I should be grateful it isn't worse, that she's not terminally ill, which I am, of course, but . . ."

Paris shakes his head. "It's still terrible. It's still a loss. A huge one, and it's still a lot of grieving and accepting something that should never have happened. You're allowed to be upset and angry about it."

I nod, barely keeping the tears at bay. "On top of everything else she got diagnosed with RA a year and a half ago. And I feel like I'm losing my mind sometimes, wondering why she can't catch a break. Why we can't."

"Fuck, I'm so sorry," he whispers and pulls me in for a hug. Tears slide down my cheeks and I don't care if people are staring, because Paris's arms around me feel so good. "Thank you for telling me."

"This isn't exactly the pick-me-up I had in mind," I murmur, and he laughs, making my chest squeeze with fondness.

"Well, it might have been what we both needed just the same."

When we get home it's beyond late because we stayed at the ice cream shop until close. Even so I'm not ready to go to sleep, or stop spending time with Paris so I ask if he's up for watching some of *The Good Place*.

He grins and nods, and even though we just had ice cream he deems popcorn being absolutely necessary and makes us some to share. It's honestly super nice to be watching it with him, and I love hearing him laugh at so many of my favorite parts. I've managed a handful of episodes over the past few weeks, but it's been by myself, and usually when I'm lying in bed at the end of a long day, ready to pass out. Sharing it with him feels good.

He giggles when I say the lines along with some of the characters since I've watched it so many times.

"You've seen this a few times then?" he says.

"What gave it away?" I ask, and wink at him.

ELEVEN

CHRIS

A few days later I'm on my way to class when my phone buzzes in my pocket. When I take it out I see it's a FaceTime call from Dad. He's not usually one to FaceTime which has me immediately concerned and the first thing that pops into my head is that something happened to Mom, so I swipe to answer it as I walk, my heart already in my throat.

"Dad?" I say when his face fills the screen. His skin is ivory and his green eyes seem more amused than scared when he smiles at me. He's got a tall, lanky frame and light brown hair parted on the side. His black framed glasses are perched on his slender nose. He's the best man I know. He's soft and gentle, but also strong and brave. He wears his heart on his sleeve. He has a soft spot for animals and a passion for gardening and landscaping, though he doesn't have a lot of spare time for either anymore. Still though, he and Mom are my heroes.

"Hey, son, we didn't want to scare you, but we thought you should know your sister is in the hospital. She's going to be just fine–"

"I broke my collar bone!" Ruby shouts offscreen, almost like she's excited about it.

"What?" I nearly shout.

Dad actually laughs. "She got a little too rambunctious during a soccer game, her and another player collided, but she's going to be fine." He angles the phone closer to the hospital bed and Ruby waves at me.

"I scored the final goal of the game though and we won so it was worth it!" Her face falls. "Except now I have to wear a stupid sling and can't play for the rest of the season."

"That sucks, munchkin, I'm sorry. Glad you're okay, though." Then I realize it's the middle of the day and Dad isn't at work because he's there with Ruby, which means, "Is Mom not feeling well?"

Dad moves the screen back to him, but he's still wearing a small smile. "No, she's been battling one of her migraines for the past couple of days. She'll be okay though."

"What about Janelle, how is she getting home from school?"

"We should be out of here soonish, but Mrs. Rodriguez is going to pick her up so I can stay with Ruby after we get home and your Mom doesn't get disturbed. We're okay, son." Mrs. Rodriguez is our next door neighbor and she's practically another grandparent. She's been there through all of Mom's health issues and watched us grow up.

"Yeah, okay," I say, though I feel guilt seeping into my pores, telling me I'm supposed to be there looking out for my family, helping them, taking care of them. And I am stressed about the fact that they now have an ER visit on top of all the other expenses.

"Listen, Dad, thanks for letting me know, I gotta get to class so I'll talk to you guys later."

"Yeah, of course. Love you, son."

"Love you!" Ruby shouts.

"Love you guys, too." I end the call and take a deep

breath, trying not to wish for the millionth time that things could be different.

When I get home that evening Paris is sitting at the table with his laptop open and is texting on his phone. The place smells amazing so I'm assuming he was cooking recently. My stomach rumbles and I smile genuinely for probably the first time that day. Just the sight of him makes some of my worries seem not so big and I find myself relaxing a smidge as I take my jacket and shoes off and make my way towards the kitchen.

"Hey," he says, though he seems a little distracted. "Dinner is in the fridge. Hope you like spaghetti."

I start rummaging through the fridge when I hear, "Shucks." Then turn to see him pouting and setting his phone down.

"Everything okay?" I ask as I dish myself some spaghetti.

He sighs. "Yeah, it's fine. I was supposed to be going to drag night at a local bar with Trent and Vanessa but they backed out."

I frown as I sit and start scarfing down my meal. "How come?"

"Vanessa is sick, and Trent said he's 'meeting with his professor'." He puts it in finger quotes. "Whatever that means. I could go by myself but I really didn't want to."

He looks super disappointed, and I find myself saying, "I could go with you, if you want." We haven't seen much of each other since the ice cream shop and spending time with Paris is never a hardship. In fact, lately, I find myself craving time with him.

"Really?" he says, his gaze shooting up to meet mine. "You don't need to be doing homework or something?"

I shrug. I should be, yes, but god, I need this. I need normal. I need fun. I need him.

"I mean, if you're sure, that would be amazing," he says, his eyes lighting up. "We'd have to leave in an hour."

"I'll finish eating and then shower. Sound good?"

He nods. "I'll go get ready."

I shovel the rest of my dinner in my mouth, put my dishes in the dishwasher, and head for the bathroom. I shower, letting the warm water soothe my aching muscles, then step out and wrap a towel around my waist, before padding down the hall to my room.

I dress in a semi-sheer, red, long-sleeved top that has black roses embroidered on it, and black leather pants. It's been a long time since I dressed up and I find I miss it. My hair is short enough that there's not really much to do with it. After brushing my teeth and applying deodorant I grab a pair of nicer shoes and slip them on.

"Wow," I hear, and turn to see Paris standing in my doorway. My jaw nearly hits the floor and whatever he's saying doesn't reach my ears because I'm too busy staring at him in the bright pink mini skirt, crop top and black knee high boots he's wearing. White fish net tights cover his slender legs, and his belly button ring is a star. His jacket is faux fur, also cropped, and very, very pink. His make-up matches to a T, and so does his purse.

"Huh?" I say, coming back to myself.

He giggles and it makes my dick twitch. Jesus fuck. *Preston's little brother*, I remind myself. *Friends.*

"I said you look really nice."

"Thank you." Why is my voice suddenly an octave deeper? I clear my throat. "Thank you," I try again. "You look amazing, too."

He blushes and gives me that amazing Paris smile. "Thank you. Ready?"

I nod, and grab my jacket on our way out the door.

When we reach Paris's Mini Cooper (also pink) I hold the driver's side door open for him and his cheeks pinken. I know it's not a date but he still deserves to be treated like a princess. "Thank you," he murmurs, and slides in.

He tells me to turn on some music for the drive and I decide to go with Tracy Chapman. My chest squeezes when he tells me he's listened to her a fair bit since I mentioned her when he moved in. I love that he took an interest in something that mattered to me. That he was curious about it. He smiles when I tell him about Mom and how much she loves her songs.

The bar is one I've never been to, and I assume he hasn't either, but it looks like there's quite a few people showing up for drag night when we pull into the parking lot.

When we climb out of the car I offer Paris my arm and he takes it, his purse over his shoulder and a mega watt smile on his face.

God, he's pretty.

It's not a huge place, which I actually like. It seems intimate and warm, and friendly. The bar is the first thing you see when you walk inside and beyond that, farther into the room are several tables with chairs, a couple of couches, armchairs, and in front of them, a stage with a red curtain behind it. Soft music plays from the speakers as we find an empty table and take our seats.

There's servers moving around delivering drinks and baskets of finger food to select tables and checking on others, taking orders.

On the walls are framed portraits of drag queens and kings, alone and in groups, as well as with patrons. Pride flags decorate the walls as well, and an amazing sense of welcome, family, and belonging sweeps over me.

"Pretty cool, huh?" Paris says, and I nod.

"You ever been here before?" He shakes his head, and I find myself liking the fact that I'm the first to share this with him.

The lights on the floor dim and the stage lights go up as one of the employees makes their way on to the stage to announce the first performer, Queen Bee.

I've seen drag in movies and tv, but I've never been to a show in person, and I find myself being swept away in it. The talent is incredible. There's singing, lip syncing, and comedy, which has both Paris and I laughing so hard our sides are splitting. But there's also a lot of heart and soul as the performers remind us of the power of diversity, individuality, challenging societal norms and embracing freedom and resistance.

The last performance of the evening is a group of queens lip syncing to "Bad Romance" by Lady Gaga and it gets a standing ovation.

Afterwards Paris asks a few of the performers if he can get a picture with them, and they happily oblige, giving him several compliments on his outfit during the process that have him beaming and blushing like crazy.

"You have fun?" Paris asks as we make our way home.

"Yeah, it was amazing. Thanks for letting me tag along. You ever think about doing drag?"

"I don't think so, though I might be convinced in the right circumstances. It's incredible to watch and I love it, but I'm not huge on performing in front of people and I really can't sing. Besides," he grins at me. "I'm a princess, not a queen."

I laugh and ruffle his hair.

PARIS

"Okay, let me get this straight," Vanessa says as we eat lunch in the student union after spending the morning attending different LGBTQ workshops together on campus. There have been a slew of informational sessions, panels, and interactive sessions over the weekend involving queer topics, like queer history, terminology, the importance of pronouns and how to use them, discussing trans and non-binary issues, advocacy and safety, including how to intervene when encountering harassment or bullying, and health and sexual wellness. It's been amazing, and a lot of people from the community have attended, too, not just those on campus.

There's a lot of topics that didn't even get discussed and so many more workshop opportunities for the future that I can't wait to do it again, and maybe even be a part of it next time. I'm not a speaker by any means, and wouldn't really feel comfortable being part of a panel, but if they did something that was more hands-on where I could do a small workshop on make-up or nails or something, that would be super fun.

"Maybe not the best word choice," Trent deadpans, and we all laugh. Vanessa smacks Trent and he mock glares at her.

"Since you broke up with Jeremy you've now gone on two," she holds up her fingers, "dates with Chris, the guy you are madly in love with."

"I'm not in love with him," I lie. I'm so fucking in love with him. If dating Jeremy taught me anything it's that what I feel for Chris isn't going away any time soon, and I'm honestly sick of fighting it. I know he doesn't feel that way about me, and I'm trying, damn it, but it's so fucking hard when every time I'm with him he just makes me love him a little bit more. I felt so honored when he shared what was going on with his family, and the care and concern he has for them just made butterflies explode in my stomach and my heart pitter patter like crazy. I hated hearing how much they are struggling and how hard it's been for them for so long. It's clear they're close, like I am with my family, and that he's desperate to try and make things better for them.

He's kind and compassionate, sweet and gentle, and so fucking sexy. God, I want him so bad. I want to know what it would feel like to kiss him for real, for him to kiss me back because he wants to. To feel his tongue against mine, to know what he tastes like. I want to know what it would feel like for those big strong hands to be on me, in me, his body pressed close to mine. I want him surrounding me, enveloping me, consuming me, in every way possible, and reminding myself that that's never going to happen is excruciatingly painful.

"And they weren't dates," I add, when Vanessa and Trent exchange glances. "He took me out for ice cream because I was upset and he wanted to cheer me up. And the other thing was because you two poopheads abandoned me and he felt sorry for me."

"Maybe," Vanessa says, sipping on her drink. "Maybe not."

I groan and roll my eyes. "He's my friend. That's it. End of story."

"Okay," Vanessa says, fiddling with her straw.

"Also, drag night was amazing and you two missed out. You're going next time." I point my finger at both of them in turn.

"I'm sorry, okay, I had a fever. And I was snotting all over everything," Vanessa says. "Trust me, you didn't want me there."

"Ew," Trent mumbles. "I'm eating."

"And you," I turn to him. "How did whatever the hell you were doing with your professor go?" I raise an eyebrow at him, still feeling like that needs some explaining.

He keeps his eyes on his food and says, "Fine."

Grrr. I want to smack him, too, but I'm not close enough. I glance at Vanessa and she smacks him for me.

"Hey," Trent squawks. "Again? Really?"

"We want answers," Vanessa says.

"Spill," I add.

Trent glares at us. We groan. God, he's so hard to read sometimes, and he's definitely a closed book. It's so frustrating. Especially since I'd give anything to hear about someone else's love life right now and not the lack of mine.

We finish our lunch and say goodbye, and since the workshops are over I make my way back to my apartment to get started on homework.

When I get home, the apartment feels so dismal and I hate the idea of sitting in it by myself, so I grab my laptop and a couple of my textbooks, shove them in my bag and head back out to my car.

When I get to *Spill the Beans* and see Chris behind the counter I can't help the smile that splits my face. My chest warms when he sees me and gives me one of his own beautiful smiles, his dark eyes lighting up.

"Hey, Pip, what are you doing here?" he says. He chuckles at himself. "Getting coffee, I suppose?"

I nod. "And saying hi to you." I fill him in quickly on my morning and the workshops, leaving out the stuff with Trent and Vanessa at lunch, before I order my drink. I snag a small table near the window, breathing in the scent of pumpkin and nutmeg that wafts up from my pumpkin spice latte. It's getting colder out as we get closer to Halloween and it's the perfect treat.

It's busier today than usual and the sounds of quiet chatter fill the space around me: the tapping of keys on a keyboard, the grinding of the coffee beans, the hiss of steam.

I retrieve my laptop and open it up, getting ready to go over some of the slides for my upcoming psychology exam.

It's not until I'm turning the cup in my hand, day dreaming, and happen to glance down that I see the name on it.

Pip. And a smiley face.

I grin and look towards the counter. Chris is busy helping another customer so I don't try to grab his attention.

A few minutes later someone joins me and I look up to see Chris smiling at me from across the table.

"Hey," he says, that grin on his face that I adore.

"Hey," I reply.

"So, I have something I wanted to ask you," he starts, and he seems a little nervous.

"Okay," I say, my heart leaping up to my throat.

"If you hate the idea or think it's silly we don't have to go."

That makes me laugh. "You're really selling it."

He chuckles. "Okay, so I found out kind of at the last minute that the local community center is hosting a ball to raise money, and I thought, I mean, if you wanted to go . . ."

Oh. My. God. I swallow even as tears fill my eyes. "You want to take me to a ball?"

His bronze skin pinkens every so slightly and he bites his lip. "I mean, I'd like to. You could be a princess in real life. Not that you aren't already, but I mean, you could dress up and everything, and it could be fun. Maybe."

"Yes," I say, wiping tears from my eyes. "That sounds amazing."

His grin is so wide it nearly stops my heart. "Great. Uh, it's in two weeks, though, does that give you enough time?"

I nod. "I'll manage."

"Okay. Good. I should get back to work." He taps the table and stands, making his way back behind the counter.

I'm gonna go to a ball with Chris.

Fuck.

TWELVE

CHRIS

The following weekend I get to sleep in. I've worked Saturday mornings for the past several weeks in a row and sleeping past 6 am. is a luxury.

When I stumble out of bed at nine I shower and dress, and then make my way into the kitchen. Only to stop dead in my tracks when I see Paris. He's dressed in pink pajama pants, a white cropped tank top, fluffy pink slippers, and his fluffy pink bathrobe. He's holding a mug in his hand, which I am assuming is full of coffee since the smell is filling my nostrils and making me crave some for myself, and he's wiping tears from his eyes.

Goddamn it. Why do those tears kill me so much? I don't like seeing anyone cry, but when it's Paris, fuck, my heart shatters every single time.

"Hey, Pip? What's going on?" I don't let him respond before I gently take his mug away and set it aside, then pull him into my arms. He wraps his arms around me and starts to sob. These sobs are nothing like the ones when he broke up with Jeremy. These are gut wrenching, full body sobs and I'm kind of freaking out while I hold him.

"I'm sorry," he blubbers after a long moment, his chest heaving against me. Then more sobs follow.

"Shh," I soothe him. "It's okay. Get it out. I'm not going anywhere."

It's several moments before he's got himself under control. He's still crying but the worst of it seems to have passed. Still, his small body is trembling and he looks exhausted.

"What's got you so upset, Pip?" I ask him, running my fingers through his hair.

"It's," he tries to get the words out as his breath hitches. "It's . . . Phoenix's . . . birthday today."

Oh, fuck.

I squeeze him tighter and he clings to me.

"Normally I'd be with my family, at least Mom and Dad. I didn't . . . " he chokes on another sob. "I didn't realize how hard it would be without them."

"I'm so sorry," I tell him. "Did you call them?"

He nods. "Yeah, it helped some. And I talked to Preston. He's gonna come over later so we can have some time together." He sniffles now and raises his head. "We used to eat his favorite dessert, and sing him *Happy Birthday* every year even after he was gone, you know? It helped, remembering him."

"That sounds like a great way to remember him." Suddenly I realize there's no reason why we can't still do that. "What if we had a party for him here this afternoon? Preston and Jackson can come, and Vanessa and Trent? We can decorate. What's his favorite dessert?"

Paris's eyes are filled with tears again, but this time I'm hoping they are happy ones. "Oh, um, butterscotch pie, which I don't know how to make. Mom always did it."

I purse my lips. "Can we get the recipe from her? I'm willing to give it a try. I haven't baked in a while but I enjoy it."

His face lights up. "Really? You'd do that?"

I'd do anything for you, I want to tell him. *Anything to see that smile.*

"Yeah, of course. He's your brother. We have to celebrate him."

He throws his arms around my neck and stands on his tiptoes, hugging me, before he plants a soft kiss on my cheek. "Thank you. I'm gonna call Preston, and then maybe we can go shopping for supplies?"

"Yeah, sounds good," I say, and watch him scamper off, my heart expanding inside my chest.

I eat breakfast and brush my teeth, and when he returns to the living room he's showered and dressed for the day and his countenance has completely shifted. I can't help the pride that fills me knowing I'm responsible for it.

"Everyone's coming, and I got them to pitch in for pizza. I also got the recipe from Mom. She cried when I told her what we were doing."

"We'll have to send them pictures."

"Definitely."

We slide into our coats and shoes and head out the door to get everything we need to make Phoenix's birthday party special.

We grab ingredients for the pie and a few snacks and drinks, then head to the party aisle. There's not a huge selection, but we grab a Happy Birthday banner and some party themed plates and cups, as well as a table cloth. We even grab some birthday hats. Then we grab a few helium balloons that are birthday themed and already inflated.

"Ooh, we should have green streamers and balloons. That was Phoenix's favorite color." Paris beams as he grabs them and tosses them in the cart.

"Candles?" I suggest. He nods and grabs a pack.

"We won't be able to fit that many candles on the pie but . . ."

"Maybe five? For each member of your family? Or six, if you want to include Ginger."

He smiles. "Yeah, I like that."

We finish our shopping and make it back to the apartment. We unpack everything and get to work. Our guests will be here in a couple of hours.

We work on the pie together and then tackle the decorations. Pretty soon the apartment is filled with the smell of butterscotch and there's a birthday banner hanging on the wall above the table, the helium balloons on either side of the banner, and the green streamers are in a canopy starting from the light fixture above the table and attaching to the walls with tape. It's not fancy but it works. And it doesn't look half bad.

Once that's finished we work on blowing up all the green balloons and they lay scattered all over the floor in just a few minutes.

"I think our work here is done," Paris says, hands on his hips, admiring everything.

"We did good, Pip." I hold my hand up and he high fives me.

"Don't forget to take pictures," I remind him.

"Oh, right." He snatches his phone and is in the process of taking pictures when there's a knock on the door.

Vanessa is the first to arrive and she wraps Paris up in a big hug. Jackson and Preston are next and the two brothers step out onto the balcony for a moment to chat. I love that they are so close, but I hate that they are both missing and grieving someone they love so much.

"This is really cool," Jackson says. "Thanks for doing this. Preston and I weren't together last year at this time and it's been a rough day for him. This helps."

I nod. "You're welcome." I wonder if Jackson ever suspected my feelings for Preston. If so he hasn't said anything, which I appreciate. Truth be told I haven't really thought of Preston that way for a while now.

Trent is the last to show up, arriving along with the pizza delivery, and we get the party started. I pass out hats and Trent and Jackson both scowl at me but don't argue. Listen, I'm not a huge fan either, but it will mean something to Paris.

We eat and drink, and we talk about Phoenix. Everyone who knew him shares stories, and we even FaceTime Pam and Phil so they can join in. Everyone but Jackson and I share something, because we didn't have the privilege of knowing him, unfortunately. We laugh. We sing to Phoenix, and Preston and Paris blow out the six candles on the cake representing their family, tears sliding down their cheeks.

His parents are crying, too. We tell Pam how delicious her pie is. They tell us thank you for inviting them to the celebration.

Hours later we're still together. And I can't imagine having spent this day off doing anything else.

When Paris passes out on the sofa later that night after the party is done and we've finished watching a movie together, I scoop him into my arms and carry him to his bed.

"Thank you," he murmurs, eyes closed as I tuck him in.

"You're welcome, Pip," I murmur, then press a soft kiss to his curls before I turn off the light and close the door behind me.

THIRTEEN

CHRIS

Jesus, why am I so nervous? It's Paris. I've known him for years, I fucking live with him. We're friends, going to a ball together. I knew he would love the idea as soon as I saw it on the community center billboard and looked it up online the second I got home. It looks perfect. Dancing, dinner, live entertainment. Is it a little costly? Yes. Should I be saving my money and not spending it on lavish events with my room- mate, probably. But god, I couldn't pass this up. Not with how much he talks about wanting to be a princess and how much I know he loves dressing up. And I'm excited about spending this time with him

I took off work for this, which I don't do. I rented a tux. Jesus, what's gotten into me?

I take a deep breath as I finish tying my bow tie. I'm wearing a basic black tux, something I haven't done since high school prom. It's kind of nice getting all dolled up though.

I finish with my bow tie and adjust my sleeves. Have I mentioned I'm nervous?

I shake myself a little, take another deep breath, let it out, and head out of the room to wait for Paris. I want to go find him, see how he's doing, but I know better than that, so instead I just pace the living room until I hear his bedroom door clicking open, and then the soft swish of fabric as he makes his way down the hall.

When he stops on the other side of the living room my chest constricts at the sight of him. I should say something, but I can't fucking breathe. He's stunning, just like I knew he would be.

His dress, if you call it that, is a two piece, and yes, it's bright pink. The top is long-sleeved and lace, except for where it covers his chest and a small portion of his abdomen. There's a few inches of bare skin between the bottom of his top piece and the top of his mermaid style skirt. I'm pretty sure that's the style anyway. It hugs his hips and thighs and then flares out around his knees. And since the dress is such that his belly button is showing, he has a gorgeous tear drop piercing there. I can't actually see his shoes since they are covered by the skirt but I'm going to go out on a limb and say they're pink, too.

He has earrings in his ears that match the one in his bellybutton. His make-up is flawless, and he's smiling at me, his cheeks pink. And I know this is more than I deserve.

"How do I look?" he says, gripping his skirt and twirling for me.

I feel my throat constricting, but manage to croak out, "Like a princess."

He beams and a second later he's in my arms and I'm spinning him around the room, laughing, and wondering how on earth he got over here so fast in heels without breaking his ankle.

"Thank you. I'm so excited, and you look amazing, too, by the way."

"Thank you," I tell him, his feet back on the floor now. "And you're welcome." My heart feels too big for my chest right now, but I pull myself together and say, "You have a jacket? It's cold."

He disappears to his room, returning with his faux fur pink jacket and matching purse. I slide my jacket on, grab my keys, and we head out.

When we arrive at the hotel where the ball is taking place, we discover there's valet parking. And since we had our first snow a couple of days ago and the parking lot is filled with slush and probably ice, I don't want Paris to have to trudge through it, so I pull up to the curb and climb out as the valet opens Paris's door and helps him out. When I reach them I offer Paris my arm and hand the valet my keys.

"Have a good evening," he says, and we make our way inside, Paris holding his skirt up as we walk, his heels clipping on the pavement.

"I've never been to this hotel. It looks nice," he says, peering up at the gorgeous building. It's multiple stories and clearly high end, with a huge banner out front that reads "Community Center Gala" and the date.

When we enter there's security we have to go through, and once that's over we step into the lobby. There's a crowd of people filling the space and after we check in there's a worker directing everyone down the hall towards the ballroom where the event takes place.

"Oh, wow," Paris gasps when we step through the ornate, white double doors and into the spacious ballroom. "This is gorgeous."

He's not wrong. The carpet is a deep purple that happens to look elegant instead of outlandish. There's a huge glass chandelier in the center of the room, and a stage to the left where a jazz band is playing soft easy music. Round tables decorate the floor, covered in purple and white linen table cloths. On each table are glass vases filled with white flowers. I'm no expert but I recognize the roses, calla lilies, and hydrangeas. Even the chairs have covers over them.

There's scads of people milling about, chatting and drinking, and tables off to the side filled with items to bid on. Since I already spent more money than I should have on the tickets and the tux I'm not planning on bidding on anything, but I don't mind seeing what's out there.

There's vacation packages, meals with people who I assume are important, though I honestly have no idea. There's gift baskets, tickets to concerts and sporting events, and there's a fair amount of artwork, too, which of course makes me think of Mom.

Paris seems to notice that I become a bit more morose looking at the artwork and I feel his hand rubbing my back.

"It's really good, isn't it? I love the farmhouse."

"It is," I agree.

"I don't suppose you could show me some of your mom's work?"

I smile. "I have some pictures I can show you."

We're busy looking at the photos I have on my phone and enjoying some appetizers when a voice comes over the speakers telling us to please take our seats and that dinner will be served shortly. We find our assigned spots, sitting down with two other couples. A white man and woman who appear to be in their seventies, dressed to the nines, and another white man and woman in their forties, also impeccably dressed. They all look like this is the type of thing they do often, and that they have a lot more money than two college students.

The elderly woman smiles brightly at us and introduces herself as Maggie. Then her husband shakes our hands and says his name is Jim.

The younger couple give us their names but don't offer us their hands. Brian and Jennifer, and I've decided already that I don't like either of them, but particularly Jennifer, who seems to be unable to look away from Paris, and is frowning deeply.

The waiter comes by and delivers our meals. It's a simple roasted chicken dish but it smells and looks amazing.

"I just love your outfit," Maggie tells Paris. "I have a grandson and a granddaughter who would be so jealous of that dress. It's stunning. And it looks lovely on you."

Paris grins. "Thank you."

"Is something wrong?" Paris asks a moment later when Jennifer won't stop whispering to her husband and casting glances our way as we eat.

"No, of course not," Brian says, seeming a little flustered, but Jennifer is scowling at us.

Then Jennifer stage whispers something that has my jaw clenching.

"I just don't get it. Why is he wearing make-up and a dress? He's not a girl. He shouldn't be pretending to be one."

"He's a human being," I retort. "And he doesn't need your approval."

"Oh honey, the only one here pretending is you with that fake rack," Maggie pipes up, and I almost spit my food out. "Also, his make-up looks ten times better than yours so maybe you should take lessons."

Jennifer gasps, her hand on her ample chest and Paris has his hand over his mouth stifling a laugh.

"Well," Jennifer seethes. "I don't have to sit here and be insulted. Come on, Brian." She throws her napkin down and pushes her chair out, gripping Brian's arm and hauling him up mid-swallow. He stumbles after her and Maggie waves cheerily.

"I always love it when the trash takes itself out," Maggie chirps, and Jim chuckles, pressing a kiss to his wife's head.

"I love you," he says, so fondly it makes me smile. "Never a dull moment."

"Are you okay?" Jim asks Paris.

"I'm fine," he says. "Thank you, but you really didn't have to. It's not the first time I've heard comments like that and it won't be the last."

Maggie scoffs. "We have two queer grandchildren, and a

transgender son, and I'll be damned if I'm going to sit here and listen to some pretentious dillweed talk like that."

Paris chuckles and I rub his back. I think I was more upset than he was, but I guess he's used to it. I hate that for him, though. No one should be used to being treated like that. There's so much ignorance and prejudice in society it's disgusting. And as a biracial Black gay man I'm intimately familiar with how it feels. I've been dealing with people's bigotry and judgmental comments since I was a kid, and it always leaves a bitter taste in your mouth regardless of the brave face you put on afterwards. I just hope it hasn't ruined his evening.

"You sure you're okay?" I ask, and he nods.

As we eat we keep talking to Maggie and Jim and since Jennifer and Brian seem to have disappeared, we enjoy our meal immensely.

As we're taking part in the delicious cheesecake we've been served for dessert, a middle-aged Hispanic woman with shoulder length dark hair and a deep blue gown takes the stage and introduces herself as Maria, charity co-organizer and one of the many people who volunteer at the community center. She thanks us for coming and shares her story about how vital her local community center was growing up and all the ways it helped her. She tells us what the community center is doing now, how they're a safe space for youth, families, immigrants and the elderly community. How they provide after school activities, sports, camps, job training, fitness classes, support groups, and so much more.

When we finish the dessert and Maggie and Jim leave the table to dance, I take the opportunity to turn to Paris and hold my hand out. "May I?"

He blushes fiercely and nods, taking my hand and letting me pull him to his feet. He grabs hold of his skirt as we make our way to the dance floor.

The music is soft and slow, and as soon as I have him in my arms I feel like I'm home. He smiles up at me, his blue eyes twinkling. He looks so beautiful and happy, and I can't help wishing this moment could last forever.

"You're a good dancer," he says softly over the music.

"Thanks, my mom taught me."

"Mine, too," he replies with a smile. "I'm having a really good time. Thank you for inviting me. I've never felt more like a princess in my life. When I went to prom in high school I dressed up and went with Trent and Vanessa and it was fun, but this feels more magical. More special. And I have the world's handsomest, most amazing prince."

I blush. "Of course." I run my finger down his cheek, and find my eyes drawn to his mouth. Those plush, pouty lips that were against mine six months ago for only a second before I jerked away and ran.

God, what I wouldn't give for a second chance at that kiss.

I clear my throat and ruffle his hair instead. He chuckles.

We sway and at some point he steps closer and rests his head against my chest. "Is this okay?"

"Yeah," I manage even as my throat constricts and my heartrate speeds up. God I really hope my dick behaves because having him pressed against me is making electricity spark like a wild fire inside me. Why does he feel so good? Why does it feel so right to hold him, to touch him? To care for him? Why do I find myself wanting so much more? Why am I wondering what he tastes like? What it would be like to feel all that soft, smooth skin against mine, to pleasure him and feel him tremble against me? Why does the idea of anyone else having their hands on him make my skin crawl?

Why do I want to be the only one who ever gets to hold him this way?

FOURTEEN

CHRIS

"Come in," I hear after knocking on the office door of one of my professors, Dr. Nelson. He emailed me yesterday saying he wanted me to stop by his office to discuss something and I've been anxiety ridden ever since. I have a feeling it isn't something good.

I open the door and step inside, closing it behind me, trying not to show just how nervous I am.

"Chris, have a seat," he says in his baritone voice. He's a big man, with rich brown skin and black hair that has streaks of gray in it. His grey eyes seem more concerned than upset. He folds his large hands and places them on his desk as he looks at me through his glasses.

"I asked to speak with you because frankly, I'm concerned. I've had you as a student now for a while and you've always done excellent work, participated in class, and you've been enthusiastic. It's clear you love what you're learning and you take it seriously. However, I've begun to notice that your focus is slipping, your exam grades aren't what they used to be, and your last paper was subpar. It's not what I expect from you. I wanted to give you the chance to tell me if there's anything going on that can explain what I've seen. Or if there's anything I or the school can do to help? Anything going on on campus or at home?"

What am I supposed to say? Tell him my family's whole story? Tell him I'm working more than I'm studying? That I'm exhausted and barely holding it together, but I don't have a choice?

I shake my head. "No, sir, I'm sorry. I'll do better." I don't know how I'm going to do better except to push myself harder. Working less isn't an option.

"You're sure? We have facilities on campus to assist with students who are struggling with feeling stressed or overwhelmed."

He means therapy, and I don't fucking need therapy. It would just take up more of my time. Time I don't have.

"I'm fine," I say.

"I hope you can make some changes. You're a bright student and you have a promising future, but I know you're here on a scholarship and the way things are looking now I'm concerned about you losing it. I'm telling you now so you can fix it." He pauses. "If you change your mind about getting some assistance you can always come talk to me. I'm here to help. If you have extenuating circumstances and you need a little extra time on an assignment, let me know. I want you to succeed, Chris. I really do."

I nod, feeling sick to my stomach and like my skin is crawling with ants. I need to get out of here. Fuck, if I fuck up my scholarship there's no way I'll finish school and I'm so damn close. I've been working my butt off for this for years and I have to get into graduate school. My parents would be so disappointed if I didn't. Fuck, I'd be disappointed. I'd be miserable. They've sacrificed so much for me. I can't let them down. I just have to push myself a little bit more.

"Thank you, is there anything else?" I ask, my voice low.

"No, that's all. Just please take care of yourself. Don't be afraid to ask for help if you need it."

I nod and head for the door.

PARIS

"Hey, I'm heading out," I tell Chris.

His eyes widen when he looks at me from where he's sitting at his desk, books out and laptop open, familiar music coming from his phone, and another can of RedBull nearby. He's been doing homework for the past few hours and he looks so worn out.

"Something wrong?" I ask, as he stares at me, his gaze raking me over. I move into his room and double check everything in the mirror. I'm dressed as a bunny rabbit. A pink, kinda slutty bunny rabbit. White mesh tights with black biker boots, pink booty shorts with a fluffy bunny tail attached, a pink cropped long-sleeved top with faux fur trim around the sleeves, collar and hem, the bunny ears headband, and I've painted the nose and whiskers on my face. I think I look pretty damn good if I do say so myself.

Chris clears his throat and I see him blink through the mirror. "No, no you uh, you look great, actually."

"Oh, good. I guess I'll see you later tonight, then? I might be home late."

He nods. "Yeah, have a good time."

I don't want to push him. He's been stressed out lately, even more so than usual and I don't want to make it worse. But maybe he could use a break? "You sure you don't want to come?"

"I want to," he replies. "I just really shouldn't. I have to get this assignment done."

"Okay. Just don't work too hard."

"Yeah," he murmurs. And then in a clearer voice. "Be safe."

I smile. It's sweet that he cares so much about me. "Thanks. I will." I wave at him and grab my coat, then head out the door.

The Halloween party is at a frathouse on campus. Preston and Jackson are going, too, and they're giving me a ride. Trent and Vanessa are meeting me there.

"Nice costume, Peter Rabbit," Jackson teases when they pull up in front of the apartment and I climb in the car.

I stick my tongue out at him and he chuckles.

"Who are you guys supposed to be?" I ask. It's kinda hard to see their costumes in the dark. It looks like they're wearing all black and that's it.

Preston chuckles, "You'll see when we get there. Part of Jackson's is in the trunk."

Oh, lord, I'm not sure I wanna know now.

When we get there Preston parks the car and we climb out. Jackson moves to the trunk and pops it, and he and Preston fiddle with something large and square with what looks like some fake prongs poking out of it, securing it around Jackson's waist. When I get closer I realize Preston's costume is basically just a jumpsuit of an outlet, then my gaze pings back to Jackson and I roll my eyes. "Oh my god, a plug and socket?"

Preston grins. "It was my idea."

"Jesus Christ," I mutter. "I'm going inside so no one sees me with you two perverts."

They both laugh. "Have fun little bro!" Preston shouts. "Don't do anything I wouldn't do!"

I shake my head and saunter inside, texting my friends to let them know where I am.

I find Vanessa and Trent out by the bonfire, roasting s'mores. It's cold, but no snow on the ground currently, and the fire is crackling, flames licking into the air. It smells like marshmallows, smoke, and ash, and it's strangely comforting.

Trent is Dr. Strange, and honestly looks super cool. Even managed to tame his hair, and Vanessa is Wonder Woman.

"I guess I missed the super hero memo," I say as I join them.

"Oh my god, you look amazing!" Vanessa cheers. She

flicks my bunny tail. "I love it. And there are some fine men here tonight, my friend. You might meet the man of your dreams."

I've already met the man of my dreams, I want to say. But I know better. I know better than to even think it. God, I'm so fucked up.

"You guys look super cool," I tell them. Vanessa beams and I think I catch the hint of a smirk on Trent's lips as he spins the stick the marshmallow he's roasting is on.

We have one s'more each and then head inside for warmth and drinks. The house is packed, and lively music fills the space, guests laughing, chatting, and dancing on the makeshift dance floor, aka, the living room, where the furniture has been pushed aside. Couples are making out in the corners and against the walls. One couple I recognize.

"Oh my god!" Vanessa cackles. "Is that your brother?"

I groan. "Jesus Christ."

"That's hot," Trent monotones as we all three watch Preston getting his face sucked by his boyfriend. Jackson has his, um, plug, shifted to the side so he can get close to Preston, and trust me they are plenty close.

I glare at Trent. "That's my brother."

He shrugs. "Still hot."

I roll my eyes and we make our way to the dance floor.

CHRIS

It's past midnight when the door to the apartment opens, and when I hear Paris talking to someone my curiosity gets the best of me and I make my way into the kitchen where I can hear him at the front door, along with a voice I don't recognize. I make sure to stay out of sight as they talk. Look, I know it's messed up, but I never claimed to be a good person.

"Thanks for walking me up. I'll see you tomorrow night, then."

"Yeah. I look forward to it."

Fuck. My stomach roils at the sound of the other voice, and the knowledge that Paris has what sounds like another date. Of course he does. He's beautiful, smart, funny. Any guy would be lucky to date him. There were probably dozens of guys at that party who wanted him. God, especially in that damn costume. He looks so fucking sexy in it. I wanted to pull him into my arms and kiss the fucking life out of him when I saw him in my doorway dressed like a slutty bunny. I wanted to rip those clothes off of him and make him mine. Fucking hell, I still do. Working on my homework instead of jerking off to thoughts of Paris took all of my willpower.

Jesus Christ. The thought of him going out with this other guy, who ever the fuck he is, is making my hackles rise.

"Goodnight," I hear Paris say, and wait until he's closed the door before I move out from behind the wall blocking me from sight.

"Hey," I say. "You're back."

"Hey," he says, seeming a bit flustered. "Yeah, just got in."

"You have a good time?"

"Yeah, a really good time. You finish your homework?"

I nod. "About twenty minutes ago."

"Well, I'm pooped. I uh, I have a date tomorrow night," he gestures at the door. "With a guy I met at the party. But maybe we can hang out before that if you're free?"

I nod. "I have a few hours in the morning. Then I'm working."

"I'll make breakfast, huh?"

I try to smile and somewhat succeed. "It's a date."

He blushes and grins. "Goodnight."

"Night, Pip," I murmur as he walks away, that fluffy bunny tail driving me insane.

FIFTEEN

CHRIS

I wake up to Paris making eggs, bacon and pancakes, and my stomach rumbles. There's coffee brewing and he's wearing his penguin onesie, looking as adorable as ever.

Every part of me aches to touch him, to hold him. To run my fingers through his hair for real. To tug on it and hear what gorgeous noises he makes when I do. I want to unzip that ridiculous, adorable onesie and see what sexy as hell panties he has on underneath. I want to lavish his small body with kisses. God, everything in me wants him in every possible way. I have nothing, though. Nothing to offer him. And I'd made it clear I wasn't interested in him that way. Would he want anything to do with me?

"Hey," he says, giving me that Paris smile. "Food's almost ready. You sleep okay?"

I'm unable to speak, apparently, so I nod.

He tells me more about his night out while we eat together. Everything tastes delicious, of course. Paris is an excellent cook. The bacon is crispy, the eggs and pancakes are fluffy, and the coffee is perfection.

He tells me about Preston and Jackson's Halloween

costumes which makes me snort, but when he gets to the part about the guy he met on the dance floor who gave him a ride home and asked him out, I have trouble unclenching my jaw. My hand is gripping my fork tighter and I feel my body growing tense.

Paris doesn't seem to notice. "Anyway, he seems nice. I don't really have much in the way of expectations, though, so we'll see."

I nod, barely registering his words.

We clean up and then he suggests playing *Mario Kart* again which does help get me in a little better mood before I head to work. He's always so animated when we play I can't help smiling and laughing at his antics.

Work itself is torture, though. I'm so fucking distracted thinking about him being on that date tonight, and the more I think about it the more sick I feel.

I take my phone out and text him.

What time is your date?

I'm meeting him at eight. Why?

Just curious if I'll be home before you leave. Fortunately I will be. I know I have no right to say anything to him, to tell him how I'm feeling. He's my best friend's brother. Six months ago I thought of him as a little brother myself. Hell, two months ago I did. But things have changed. I've changed.

And I want him.

God, I want him so badly.

But what if it's too late?

PARIS

That was weird. Chris asking when my date is. I shrug it off though, and focus on my homework until six o'clock rolls around and it's time for me to get ready. I've been lounging around in my bunny onesie all day after showering. I'm definitely ready to get out of the apartment, though, even if I am a little nervous.

Chris comes in the door just as I'm standing up from the table and stretching. He seems a little off. A little nervous, maybe? But I can't imagine why.

"Hey, you okay?" I ask.

"Uh, yeah, sure," he mutters, kicking his shoes off and shrugging off his coat. He fidgets with his keys and stares at me.

"Okay," I say, drawing the word out. "Well, I'm gonna go get ready. I made you some dinner. It's in the fridge."

He nods as I saunter towards the hall. I've got my hand on the bathroom door, ready to go inside when I hear, "Don't go out with him." It's so soft I wonder if I actually heard it.

I blink and turn. What? I can't have heard him correctly. Why would he say that?

I make my way back down the hall slowly. Chris is still standing near the door, keys in his hand. He drops them in the basket by the door and shoves his hands in the pockets of his jeans. He swallows. He won't stop fidgeting, and he's breathing heavier than normal.

"What?" I whisper, my own heart rate picking up.

He takes a step closer. And then he says it again, clear as day. "Don't go out with him. Please."

I blink again, trying to register his words. I feel slightly dizzy. And incredibly confused. "Why?" I croak out. He's even closer now.

"Because I can't stand the thought of you being with him," he says, and I swallow. I can't be hearing him correctly. This must be a dream, or an acid trip. What is happening? I feel like I'm losing my mind.

I shake my head, and I realize when my vision blurs, that I have tears filling my eyes. "I don't understand." My chest heaves. "What's happening?"

He steps closer but I take a step back, shaking my head even more.

"I know this probably feels like it's coming out of nowhere," he tells me. "But it's not. I know you could do so much better than me, Pip. But I'm fucking crazy about you, and I can't let you go on this date without telling you how I feel."

I'm sobbing now, tears streaking my cheeks. "Don't," I hiccup. "Don't. I've been in love with you for two years," I tell him. "I've spent the last nine months telling myself you don't care for me that way and trying my hardest to get over you. So if this is some kind of a joke, it's a very, very cruel one."

"No," he says, stepping closer again before I can back away. He grips my cheeks and starts wiping my tears with his thumbs. I'm shaking now. "God, no, it's not a joke, baby. I swear it's not. I'm so overwhelmed with how I feel for you, I don't even know what to do with it. I want you, Paris. I want you so damn bad I can't stand it. I want all of you. Everything. You make me so damn happy, just being with you, talking to you, spending time with you. I want your smile and your laughter and your energy. I want your heart. I want your passion and your courage. I want it all, every single day. And if you'd ever consider giving me the honor, I want your body, too. I'm so fucking in love with you, Pip."

I'm sobbing even harder now, my heart thrashing wildly against my ribcage. He loves me? He *loves* me? *He* loves *me*? And he called me baby.

"I think," I manage to croak out. "I think I need a minute. Please."

His brows furrow and a frown creases his handsome face, but he nods and lets go of me. I slip into my room and close the door behind me.

Holy shit.

SIXTEEN

CHRIS

Fuck, fuck, fuck. I pace my room for what feels like hours waiting for Paris to emerge, wondering if I've just colossally screwed up everything. I couldn't keep it in any longer, though. I couldn't keep lying to myself, telling myself I only saw him as a friend, as my best friend's little brother. He's so much more than that. He's everything to me.

I just hope I'm still something to him.

He said he'd been in love with me for two years. Jesus, I figured he felt something, attraction at the bare minimum, after that kiss. But what now? Has that faded, vanished completely? Did I wait too long to see what was right in front of me?

I'm sitting at my desk pretending to do homework, my leg bouncing as I bite my bottom lip. I'm so nervous I can't even break out my music. I know it wouldn't help. I don't regret what I did, what I said. I meant every word of it. I fucking love him. But god, I'm a wreck right now.

I nearly jump out of my seat when there's a knock on the door. Fuck, my heart is in my throat. "Come in," I say, my voice hoarse.

The door opens and Paris stands there, still in his bunny onesie, looking exhausted and like he just had the shock of his life, maybe because he did. He shuffles his foot back and forth, hands in the pockets of his jammies, then he shuffles forward, a flush on his face.

"Hi," I say. "Are you okay?"

He nods. "Are you?"

I nod. "If you want to pretend like nothing happened–"

"I canceled my date," he blurts.

I blink. "Oh." Then a smile breaks out across my face as he shuffles closer, looking cuter than hell in that bunny onesie. "Yeah?"

He nods, a grin spreading across his face now. "Yeah."

He's close enough now he's pressed against my knees. I spread my legs wider and he steps closer. My hands grip his hips. His hands grip my face. My eyes fall to his lips at the same time his eyes fall to mine.

"I'd really like you to kiss me right now," I murmur.

He grins and a single tear slides down his cheek. "Will you kiss me back this time?" he asks with a shaky laugh.

I nod. "I promise."

Then his lips meet mine, and the second they do I'm gripping him tighter, pulling him closer. He gasps and straddles my lap as my arms come around him. God, it's so much better than I imagined. His lips are so soft and full and his body is warm and feels just right against me. He whimpers when I slide my tongue over his bottom lip and the sound goes straight to my dick. Then he's opening for me, and we're both moaning as my tongue slides along his. He shivers in my arms and I groan, my hands sliding down to grip his round little ass.

Fuuuuck. Another groan leaves me, my cock rock hard as he tilts my head back, deepening the kiss. He tastes like sugar and strawberries and I can't get enough.

"Is this okay?" I ask, my voice husky, hands still gripping his ass. He nods and tries to scoot even closer. Fuck. His lips find mine again and we're kissing each other slow and deep. It's intimate and so fucking perfect. Our hands explore, running along each other's sides, and chests, and up each other's arms and through each other's hair. God, his hair is so soft, and when I give it a tug he lets out the most glorious whimper and his mouth parts, letting me delve inside even deeper. Every brush of his lips against mine, every swipe of his tongue, every touch has my body reacting, my need for him intensifying.

Jesus, the noises he makes are enough to make me come undone. My dick is leaking obscenely in my briefs and I moan when I feel his dick brush against mine through the fabric of our clothes.

"Jesus fuck," I gasp, pulling back. "Fuck, baby." My chest is rising and falling rapidly and so is his. His face is flushed, his eyes hooded, his perfect lips swollen and puffy, hair wild, my hand still gripping it. God, he looks obscene, and I fucking love it.

"Paris?" I try to calm myself, but I don't know how that's possible with him so close, smelling so sweet and tasting like sin. God, he's everything. "Tell me what you want. I don't want to do anything you don't want me to do."

He bites his lip, his thumb running over my bottom lip. "What do you want to do?" he asks, his gaze meeting mine, and my dick bucks, my grip on his hair and his ass tightening.

"I'm kind of afraid to say," I admit, my voice raspy. He whimpers and ruts against me and I growl. "I might scare you off."

He giggles and leans forward. "Tell me," he whispers in my ear, then nibbles on it.

"I want to take you apart," I tell him as he plants kisses on my neck and jaw, making me shudder. "I want to get this onesie off of you and I want you underneath me. I want to make you mine. I want to fill you up so full. I want to worship you. I want you begging me. I want you desperate. I want to see that pretty cock of yours leaking, and I want to see what you look like when you come with my name on your lips."

He pulls back, staring at me, eyes wide. "Fuck." He kisses me hard and long and deep, rutting against me as he does, his dick jerking against mine and making me quake with desire. "Take me to bed," he demands. "Fuck, Chris. I want you so bad."

I grip his thighs and stand, carrying him with me to the bed and laying him down, hovering over him on my hands and knees. We kiss again for several more seconds before I pull away and stare down at him. "Are you sure?" I ask, even as my dick throbs. "I know this is a big deal for you. I don't want–"

"Chris," he interrupts. "I've never been more sure of anything in my life. You're the only one I want this with. Please fuck me. Make me feel good."

God, the way he's looking at me is enough to make my heart melt. He really wants this. Wants me to be his first.

I nod.

"Just be gentle," he says, his cheeks flushing.

I grip his chin in my hand and kiss him. "Of course, princess."

His eyes light up, and he smiles, then starts to squirm. He tugs on my shirt and I take the hint and strip it off, tossing it to the floor. He stares at me, his small pale hand moving over the rose tattoo on my left pec, down my torso, his fingers tracing the outline of my abs. He shivers and his gaze finds mine again. "You're so beautiful. I can't," he sucks in a breath and tears fill his eyes. "I can't believe you want me. I can't believe . . . "

"Shh," I say, and kiss him again. I wipe his tears. "I'm the lucky one here. I can't believe I get to have you, Pip. And just in case it wasn't clear before, this is not a game for me. This is not a trial or casual fling. I know people generally date for a while before they make love confessions, but I wasn't exaggerating earlier when I said how I felt about you. I'm crazy about you. I love you. I love you so much it hurts."

He smiles. "I love you, too."

"What have you done?" I ask, while peppering kisses along his neck and jaw. He tastes so sweet it's driving me crazy. I'm desperate to get him naked. I reach for the zipper on his onesie and start to tug it down, slowly revealing inch after inch of smooth, pale skin. He bites his lip.

"Nothing," he says softly, and my eyes meet his.

"Nothing?" I repeat, my hand stilling. He squirms.

"Is that okay?" His cheeks are flushed and he looks so damn beautiful beneath me. But he's clearly nervous, too. Like he's afraid I'll reject him for his lack of experience. Nothing could be further from the truth.

I shake my head. "Yes, of course. But just to be clear, when you say nothing . . . "

"I mean nothing," he says. "No handjobs, blowjobs, nothing. I've only ever kissed the guys I've been with. I mean I've masturbated but nothing with anyone."

I can't help it. I smile. He blushes even deeper. I kiss him. "I'm gonna make you feel so good, princess. I promise. I'm gonna take such good care of you." I start to unzip his onesie again and his breathing picks up, his erection growing and tenting his jammies by the time the zipper reaches his belly button. I move the onesie aside and press kisses to his bare skin. He shivers and sweet little whimpers leave his lips, my name on his tongue.

"Up," I tell him, when I've reached his pelvis and need more. He sits up and yanks the sleeves off, then lies back down and lifts his hips so I can grip the onesie and pull it down his legs.

My dick bucks when I see his cock tenting his pretty, pink, lace panties, and my mouth waters. I've never seen anything so sexy in my life, and the fact that there's a wet spot forming on them already is even better. Fuck, he's hard for me. Hard and leaking. Goddamn, I'm about to lose my mind.

"Jesus Christ," I whisper, my voice low and raspy as I chuck the onesie aside and stare at him. "You have no idea how much I've wanted to see you like this." I lean forward and press more kisses to his bare skin, working my way up his body, his belly, his torso, his chest, then along his neck as he gasps and grips my arms, spreading his legs to let me slot between them.

"These panties are so fucking sexy," I rumble as he shivers against me. "You're so damn sexy, princess."

"Chris," he whines, bucking his hips up into me. I groan at the friction of his cock against mine even through my jeans. "Please."

I slide off the bed and strip out of my jeans, but leave my boxer briefs on for the time being. Then I'm back on the bed, hovering over him. "I want to fuck you," I tell him, "but not yet, okay? I want to take my time. I want to make you come at least once before I'm inside you. Is that okay?"

He nods. "Yes," he says in a breathy whisper. "Please."

I kiss him again and he whimpers when my tongue tangles with his. A moan escapes me and my dick throbs, a sizable wet spot forming. I suck and nibble and lick on his neck and he whines, bucking up into me again and saying my name over and over. It's music to my ears.

When I take his ear in my mouth and start to play with it, he wails and his body jerks. Holy shit. "Good to know, princess," I murmur. "You like this?" I suck on his ear lobe, then slide my tongue along it and he quakes, his body shaking as his hands grip my hips and he thrusts up against me again, seeking friction.

"Fuck, Chris. Touch me. Please. I want it so bad."

I play with his ear a little bit longer, then kiss down his body once again, making my way to his groin. I nuzzle his dick through his panties, feeling his precum against my skin as I breathe him in. I keep nuzzling him. God, he smells so sweet.

He gasps and whimpers as I move my nose along his

shaft. It's not particularly big but it's just right for him. I press kisses to his dick through his panties, cupping it gently in my hand as I do.

"Fuck, Chris, fuck," he whines, shoving his dick into my face, his hand on my head.

I hum and move my hand down, then start to roll his balls as I kiss his dick over and over. Playing with him like this is turning me on so fucking much. I can't get enough.

I growl when his dick twitches against my lips again and again. It's so damn hot. I tug on his sack and he squirms.

"Fuck, that's so good," he whimpers.

I grip his shaft in my hand as I stare at him, his skin flushed, eyes dark, chest rising and falling in heavy breaths, forehead beaded in sweat, nipples hard. He's so damn beautiful. I start to stroke him through his panties and he lets out a shout. I keep my eyes on his perfect face as his eyes close and his mouth falls open. His small hands are gripping the sheets now and he's chasing my hand, thrusting into it.

"God, you're perfect," I murmur, planting a kiss on his ribs. "I want you to come just like this for me, baby. You okay with that?"

He nods. "God, I'm so close, Chris."

I stroke him faster as my mouth finds his again. I want him to come while I can feel his lips against mine, my tongue in his mouth. I want his cock pulsing and spurting in my hand so damn bad. I want to know what it feels like when he releases all that spunk for me. I'm craving it.

He whimpers and his body goes rigid. Then he's moaning into my mouth as his dick pulses in my hand, his release coating his panties. I growl and milk every last drop of his seed from his perfect cock. My mouth leaves his and I suck on his ear, making him cry out as he gifts me with another shot of his spunk.

"God, yes," I rasp when his body trembles with the after-shocks of his orgasm. The one I gave him. The one he gave to me. "Fuck, princess, that was so damn hot."

I sit up and tug his panties down. They're soaked with his spunk as is his softening cock, and my mouth waters at the sight. "Can I clean you up?"

He nods, still blissed out. I lean over and lick his seed from his dick and balls, swallowing it down and humming at the sweet, salty taste.

"Oh, fuck," he gasps, his body twitching. "That's hot."

I chuckle. "You are so damn gorgeous when you come, Pip."

He flushes bright red. "What about you?" His eyes fall to my very hard cock, straining against my briefs.

"We'll get to me in a bit," I tell him. "If you're up for more? No pressure though."

He nods eagerly.

I smile. "You think you can get that pretty cock hard for me again?"

"Definitely," he replies with a hitched breath. I kiss him and then proceed to slide his panties off the rest of the way and toss them on the floor. My breath catches at the sight of him, lying there on my bed, arms above his head, naked and sated. The only thing on his small, slender body is the gorgeous star belly button ring in his navel. He looks like seduction itself.

"Fuck, I can't get over how damn pretty you are," I murmur, sliding my hand along his torso and trailing a single finger around his belly button. I lean forward and press a kiss to his belly button ring and he shivers. Then I lie down next to him, stroking his cheek as I stare at him.

"So, how was your first handjob?" I ask.

"Amazing," he says. We kiss for a while, slow and sweet and soft, before the kisses become more heated, our bodies moving closer again as our tongues tangle and our hands roam.

He whimpers into my mouth when I tug on his curls and it goes straight to my balls.

"Need you," he whines, gasping as I grip his ass cheek

and squeeze, then pressing himself against me so our bodies are flush. "Make me yours. Wanna feel you inside me so bad."

Fuck. He grips my cock through my underwear and squeezes, making me buck and groan. I slide my finger along his dick and precum gathers on the tip. I move my finger between his ass cheeks and tap his hole, slicking it up with his precum. He whimpers and I keep my finger there, circling the tight pucker, making him shiver against me and making my own cock throb.

I move, pushing him on his back and hovering over him again, kissing him as he spreads for me. God, being between his legs is like nothing I've ever felt before. It feels so damn right.

"More," he begs, spreading his legs wide as I slide my finger along his hole, circling it. I move the pad of my finger over it again and again, slowly, and he squirms and writhes beneath me.

"I wanna see your cock," he breathes. "Please."

I kiss him and then shuck my underwear, tossing it on the floor, before I'm between his legs again. My cock is leaking obscenely now, dripping onto his stomach, and he stares at it. It's bigger than his, longer and thicker, and has a Prince Albert piercing.

"Fuck, you're pierced," he gasps. "That's so hot. Can I . . . can I touch you?"

I grin. "Of course you can." He reaches down tentatively and rubs his thumb over the piercing, then along the slit, making me suck in a breath as my dick jerks. He does it a few more times and my precum is oozing out on to his digit as my body trembles. "Fuck, Pip."

His eyes meet mine and he grins. Then his hand slides down to grip my shaft. "God, I love touching you," he says as a shudder rolls through me.

I groan as he starts to stroke me. "It's just a dick," I tease.

"And my hand is just a hand?" he asks, meeting my gaze again.

"Fuck, no," I groan. "It's everything." I press my lips to his as he continues to play with my cock, loving every single second of his hand on me.

"I want you inside me," he whimpers, after several more moments of kissing and stroking me. He moves his hand from my dick to my ass and squeezes, his other hand gripping my opposite hip.

"Soon," I promise, then grip his cock and start to stroke him slowly. "I wanna play with your pretty hole a little longer first. I like having my hand down there. Wouldn't mind my mouth down there for a bit, too, if you're okay with it."

He nods. "Yes. God, yes. Please."

I grin and kiss him as I stroke him more. I don't think I'll ever get enough of his cock in my hand, his needy whimpers and moans and the way he says "please" for me.

"Show me where you want me, then, baby," I tell him. His eyes darken and he hikes his legs up, spreading them wide, giving me the perfect view of his pretty hole. It flutters and I groan. "Is this for me?" I ask, tapping it, and he nods as he sucks in a breath. I start to circle it again. "All for me? Only mine, no one else's?" I rub one of his slender thighs as I stare at him and he shivers.

"Yes."

I hum and slide my fingers along his lips. "Get them wet for me, princess."

He takes them into his mouth and I groan as he licks and sucks, coating them in his saliva. Then they're back at his hole, and I'm leaning over him, sliding my tongue into his mouth again and reveling in how his body responds to mine, the beautiful noises pouring from his sinful lips, telling me I'm making him feel good.

I spend several moments just coating his hole in his spit, circling it, tapping it, driving him wild with need and feeling him quiver against me, him saying "please" over and over again between kisses before I finally give in and slide my finger inside him.

He gasps and instantly spreads his legs even wider. I suck and lick on his neck, sliding my dick along his as I finger him, and fuck, it's incredible. My entire body is a livewire, and I need so much more of him.

"I need to taste you," I rasp. "Keep those legs spread for me, baby." I slide my finger out of him and lower my mouth to his hole. He keens when I slide my tongue over his pucker and groan. "Oh, god." I lick and suck and nibble on his precious hole while he gasps and writhes.

"Fuck, Chris, fuck, oh fuck, fuck fuck." His words only spur me on and I slide my tongue inside, desperate for more.

"Shit!" he wails. "Oh god, fuck."

I slide out and he whimpers. "No, please."

I lift his hips and slide a pillow under him, then return to my task, eating him out viciously, shoving my tongue as far inside him as I can get and feeling him shake and tremble against me, his hole clenching and spasming around my tongue.

"Fuck, stop," he gasps. I back away, saliva dripping down my chin and coating his ass crack. His hole is red and puffy and so damn beautiful. My breaths are heavy and so are his. "I don't wanna come without your cock inside me. Please."

I nod. "You need a little bit more prep first."

I reach for the bedside table, grabbing the lube and condom. He whimpers and squirms as I slick lube over my fingers.

The little whimper mixed with the sigh of relief he lets out when my fingers find his hole again is almost enough to have me coming on the spot. I use two fingers this time, and he shakes when I enter him, but his body accepts me like I fucking belong there. "Oh, god, yes."

"You okay?" I ask, moving my fingers slowly inside him. He nods.

"It feels so good."

I press kisses to his skin as I stretch him, then suck the tip of his cock into my mouth at the same time that I nudge his sweet spot. He shouts, his back bowing. "Fuck! Oh, holy shit. More."

I pop off his dick and focus on his prostate, nudging it repeatedly and watching him fall apart. "Please, please, please," he whines. "Fuck, please fuck me. I need your cock. Please, Chris." Goddamn, I still can't get over how badly he wants me.

I slide my fingers out and press a kiss to his lips. Then I'm slipping the condom on and coating my cock in lube.

As soon as the head of my dick comes in contact with his hole he lets out something between a moan and a whine, then gasps when I breach him. "You okay?" I ask again, one hand planted beside him, the other rubbing circles on his tummy.

He nods.

"I've got you," I tell him. "I won't hurt you, baby. I promise." I kiss him and he whimpers as I slide inside him a bit more. I deepen the kiss and push just a little bit more inside. I did a good job prepping him and his body welcomes the intrusion. It's tight, and so damn hot. "Fuck, Pip, you feel good." I pull out almost all the way, and he whimpers, his hands gripping my biceps as he shakes his head and his legs tighten around me.

"Don't go."

I chuckle and kiss him. "I'm not going anywhere, baby. Just letting you adjust." I push back in slowly, all the way to the hilt, and when I bottom out I close my eyes and take a deep breath, my forehead resting against his. Fuck, he feels amazing. My body trembles as I adjust to the feel of him choking my dick with his sweet hole. To the knowledge that I'm inside him. Jesus Christ, I'm inside him. Holy fuck.

I hear his breath hitch and my eyes open to see tears sliding down his cheeks. "You okay?" I ask, terrified for a second that I might have hurt him or that he's changed his mind.

He nods. "Just, fuck . . ." his breath hitches. "Fuck, you're inside me. I can't believe you're inside me. I can't . . . "

I kiss him again. I don't think I'll ever get enough of his soft, pillowy lips. "I know," I say. "I know. Me either. God, I'm so ready though. I want to make you feel good, Pip. Can I move?"

He nods, and I start to thrust slowly. His legs tighten around me and he kisses me as I move. Not fast and hard but slow and deep, drawing the most incredible noises out of him. I don't want to fuck. I want to make love to him. I want to show him just how much he means to me. I want this to be everything he deserves and more.

"Oh, fuck, Chris," he gasps against my lips. "Fuck, baby, that's good." I change my thrusts so they're a little deeper as I kiss and suck on his ear and he clings to me and moans. God, I want to stay inside him forever.

"Oh, oh, oh," he whimpers when I nudge his prostate again and again, moving my hand to his nipple to play with it as I continue to suck on his ear. He's shaking underneath me, and his smooth skin feels incredible against mine, his ass so perfect around my cock and his cock pressed between us, leaking like a sieve.

"Oh, fuck, Chris." He babbles as I pleasure him. "I'm close. I'm so close. Your cock is amazing."

I hum in his ear and then grip his dick in my hand and stroke him in tandem with my thrusts as I continue to play with his ear. He's shouting seconds later and his perfect cock is pulsing in my hand, stream after stream of cum shooting out and onto his abdomen and chest. It's the most beautiful thing I've ever seen and it makes my own orgasm barrel up on me. I'm crying out seconds later and filling the condom deep inside him as his own body trembles with aftershocks.

"Oh god," he breathes, as I collapse on top of him. "Fuck." His arms and legs are holding me to him and he's sobbing.

"Shh," I soothe, planting kisses on his cheeks and wiping away his tears. "Did I hurt you?"

He shakes his head. "God, no, it was perfect. Fuck, it was so perfect. I'm sorry, I honestly don't know why I'm crying."

I smile. "It's okay. Don't apologize." I kiss him again. "I love you."

He smiles. "I love you, too. I think that's why I'm crying. Because we actually had sex and it was so much better than I ever thought it would be, and it was you. God, it was you. It's just . . . wow." He laughs even as more tears slide down his cheeks. I don't blame him. It's a lot to take in, and for someone who cares so much about sex being special, it makes sense it's making him emotional.

Fuck, he's so perfect. How did it ever take me so long to see that? My heart swells at how much love I have for him. It's almost overwhelming.

I pull out of him and toss the condom in the trash, then grab the wipes from the nightstand to clean him off. He blushes as I do and I press a kiss to his belly, and then one to his soft cock. He gasps and his dick twitches, which I love, so I kiss it again.

"Do you want to shower?" I ask, collapsing next to him.

"No, I'm pooped," he says. "I just want to sleep."

I nod and pull him to me. He snuggles up against me and it's so perfect I feel tears stinging at my eyes now.

"I like your tattoo," he says softly, his finger tracing over the five small roses grouped together on my pec. "It's beautiful. Is it because your last name is Rose?"

I nod. "One rose for each of us. I got it before I came to college. My mom loves roses, too, and my dad is really into landscaping and gardening. When they bought the house they planted a rose bush out front and every summer he fills the house with roses for Mom. She does a lot of them in her paintings, too, and being so far away, it helps to feel like I have a way of keeping them all close to me."

He looks up at me. "I like that. I hope I get to meet your family someday."

I squeeze him to me and kiss the top of his head. "Me, too," I say.

SEVENTEEN

PARIS

I wake the next morning to gentle fingers stroking my bare skin and soft kisses being peppered along my neck and shoulder. I moan when I feel Chris's erection against my ass. God, is this real? The pleasant ache in my backside tells me it most definitely is, but I'm still trying to process it all.

Chris loves me. He's in love with me. Something I never thought would happen has, and fuck, I'm overjoyed. Last night was incredible. He took such good care of me. I can't imagine my first time being with anyone other than him. He was so gentle, and sweet, but so passionate, too. Sex with Chris is everything I thought it would be. It was perfect. And god I want more. More of him. More of us. I want to keep falling in love with him every single day for the rest of forever. I want to care for him, support him, make him laugh and smile, and hopefully have so, so many more orgasms like the one he had last night.

But there's still one question nagging at my mind and I have to know.

"Morning, princess," he purrs in my ear, and a shiver races down my spine. His finger plays with my belly button ring as he sucks on my earlobe. God, why does that get my engine going so damn fast?

I turn and face him, giving him a soft smile but also putting some distance between us. His eyebrows furrow and the sparkle in his deep brown eyes dims.

"What's wrong?" he asks. "Are you–"

"Are you still in love with Preston?" I blurt. His eyes widen and his body stiffens.

He sighs heavily after a moment and his shoulders relax. "Of course you knew," he says softly. "I think everyone knew except him."

He reaches over to take my hand and I let him. It's warm, and gentle, and reassuring. He looks into my eyes when he says, "No, Pip. No, I'm not still in love with him. Do you think I would have told you I loved you if I was? That I would have made love to you if I was?"

I shrug. "I mean, I'd like to think you wouldn't, but I had to know." My body is trembling now and he squeezes my hand a little tighter.

"I understand," he says. "But you're the only one I have eyes for. You have my whole heart, Pip. If you want it. I swear the feelings I did have for Preston aren't there anymore. I love him, like I always will, as a friend, but I'm *in* love with you. And I swear I wouldn't have touched you or let anything that happened between us last night happen if I still had even an ounce of feelings for your brother." He strokes my cheek and whispers, "You're my whole damn world, princess."

I nod, and a tear slips free.

"Are we okay?" God he sounds so nervous, like I might actually tell him I don't want to be with him after all.

"Yeah," I say, smiling now and squeezing his hand back. "Yeah, we're okay. We're better than okay."

Relief fills his features and he smiles. "Thank god. Can I kiss you?"

I smile wider and nod again, moving closer to him. The kiss is soft and slow and sweet, and it's just what I need.

"Can we not tell him?" I ask, when our lips part for the final time. "Preston, I mean. Can we not tell him about us yet?"

"You worried he'll be upset?"

"Maybe," I say. "I honestly don't know. I just, I don't want to risk it. This is so new and I'm so happy, and I don't want anything to ruin it. I uh, I would like to tell Trent and Vanessa, though."

"Okay," he says, stroking my cheek. "Whatever you want. I'm a little nervous about how Preston will react, too, but I hope he'll be cool with it, eventually at least, if not right away, but yeah, we can wait."

He kisses me again. "I have to shower and get ready for work."

I grin as he climbs out of bed. I don't think there's anything better than watching that firm, tawny ass as he walks out of the room and down the hall to his bathroom. I stretch, and then climb out of bed myself, blushing and smiling furiously when I see the evidence of our incredible night together; my onesie in a heap on the floor along with Chris's clothes, the used condom in the trash, and my favorite, my cum covered panties. God, he made me come twice and both times were amazing.

I grab our things and toss them in the wash on my way to my own bathroom. I brush my teeth and pee, but since I want to make breakfast before I shower so Chris can eat before he leaves, I just slide into a fresh pair of panties, white ones this time, that showcase my buttcheeks and have a heart shaped cut out in the back, and my cropped Care Bear T-shirt. I slide my fluffy pink slippers on, too, and then head into the kitchen.

I'm standing at the stove, scrambling eggs, the bacon in the oven when I hear a breathy, "Fuck, baby."

My cheeks heat and I grin when I turn to see Chris coming towards me, dressed in jeans and a gray T-shirt. His large hands land on my shoulders.

"Hi," I say, a shudder already working its way through my body.

"Hi," he says, his voice deep and raspy as his strong arms slide around me from behind and his hands roam my body. He presses soft kisses to my neck, and the sensitive spot behind my ear, making me squirm. My dick is hard and straining against my panties in an instant. "Fuck, your panties are so damn sexy, Pip. You're so damn sexy."

My brain is sort of malfunctioning at the moment and all I can manage as he caresses my skin is a garbled, "Uhh."

He chuckles, low and soft as his hand slides up my shirt and starts to play with my nipple. I jolt and drop the spatula I was using to cook the eggs. Chris reaches forward and turns off the burner as his other hand slides up and grips my throat gently. I gasp, then moan when I feel his rock hard cock against my backside. I shove my ass back against him, a pathetic whimper leaving me as the need for him to fill me again takes over.

"Oh, god," I beg, as his fingers tease my nipple and his tongue flicks my ear. I rut against him like an animal in heat. Fuck, he's going to make me come without even touching me. "Fuck, baby, I need you."

"I have to go to work," he teases, his hand tweaking my nipple in a way that makes me yelp even as my dick jerks from the pleasure.

I nearly growl, and his hand around my neck tightens a little which makes my dick throb. My clean panties are now soaked in precum, and his large hand skates down my torso torturously slowly, before it dips inside the waistband of my panties. I nearly sob in relief when he takes me in his hand and starts to stroke me slowly.

"Oh, fuck, princess, you're so damn wet for me already," he rasps, and my body shudders, my dick jerking and oozing even more precum onto his hand. I shove my ass against his crotch again and he sucks on my ear as his thumb plays with the slit of my dick.

"Fuck, Chris, please," I beg, humping his hand and thrusting back against his cock like a fucking slut. God, I feel like I'm going to lose my mind if he doesn't get that big, beautiful dick inside me right fucking now.

"You want something, gorgeous?" he asks. His hand moves from my throat to my hair and he tugs, sending a jolt of pleasure straight to my cock. I whimper.

"I want your dick," I tell him, my head resting against his shoulder. "Please?"

He presses kisses to my neck as he strokes me. "Tonight," he says, and I nearly scream. "I'll fuck you so good tonight, princess. But right now I want you to do something for me."

I squirm as his hand plays with my dick. "What?" I ask.

"Show me how fucking pretty you look when you come in your panties. I fucking need it, baby. Give me this. Fill these pretty panties for me. Soak them in your cum and I'll fuck you so damn good tonight you'll see stars."

Oh fuck. My prince has a fucking filthy mouth, and I think I love it. I nod, whimpering, and he strokes me faster, sucking on my ear and tugging my hair which apparently both really rev my engine because I am so damn close already.

"Nnnnnn," I moan, eyes closed and head tilted back in bliss as he pleasures me. The fact that he's making me come, and that I'm giving him something he wants is making this that much hotter. "Oh, fuck, Chris. Fuck, baby."

"You gonna come for me?" he rasps. I nod.

"Oh god!" I shout as my release barrels up on me. His hand feels so damn good on my cock, his sinful mouth on my ear, sucking and licking, sending me over the edge in a fucking freefall. My cock pulses as I cry out and my panties are soaked with my release in seconds, aftershocks rolling through my body in waves.

He holds me to him as I shake and my breathing evens out. "Goddamn, Pip," he murmurs in my ear. "You're so fucking perfect. That was fucking gorgeous, baby."

I preen at his words because apparently I'm a slut for

praise. He notices because as soon as the words leave his mouth my cock is twitching in his grip, and he hums, kissing my neck again. Then he's sliding his hand out of my panties and I can't help grinning when I see that it's coated in my spunk.

Instead of walking to the sink and washing his hand, though, he starts licking the cum off his hand like it's the best thing he's ever tasted. He does wash them after that, but by then I'm trying to keep from getting hard all over again. God, I love that he wants to taste me. I thought last night when he licked up my spunk might have been a fluke but apparently not.

"I should get going," he says, then presses a kiss to my lips. "Thanks for making my morning."

"But, what about breakfast?" I ask.

He grins. "I had mine."

EIGHTEEN

CHRIS

I don't stop smiling the entire day at work. Even when one of my coworkers calls out sick and I'm scrambling to prepare orders. Even when a customer yells at me for not having the pastry she wants even though we only offer them in the morning and it's past noon. And even when I have to remake a drink three times because the customer insists it's not "mocha enough". For the record I don't do anything differently with the drink but they seem appeased with the final attempt.

I'm on cloud nine and I don't think anything could bring me down. And the fact that I'm texting Paris when there's a lull and he responds right away makes it even better.

How's my princess? I ask him.

Horny and happy, he replies, and I grin and chuckle, my dick twitching in my pants. *I told Vanessa and Trent.*

And?

Vanessa shrieked and about burst my eardrums. Trent was Trent.

I know what that means. His friend is as stoic a person as I've ever met. He probably mumbled "Cool" and that was it.

I miss you, I tell him.

Miss you, too. Can't wait for you to get home. I've been thinking about that promise you made me all day.

I groan and have to stop myself from adjusting my dick, which is getting harder and harder the longer we talk. And even though I know it's a terrible idea I type, *You mean the one where I promised to fuck you so good you saw stars?*

God, you can't say that. Now I'm hard. Well, harder. I've been half hard since you left.

Fuck, he's going to ruin me. *Jesus, baby, I'm trying to work here,* I tell him.

He sends a lip biting emoji.

What are you doing? I ask.

Homework.

I can't help it. *What are you wearing?*

Come home and find out, my handsome prince.

I nearly growl but stop myself before it slips out. That's when the bell above the door jingles.

Gotta go. See you later. Love you.

Love you, too, handsome. Kissy face emoji.

I finish work a few hours later and they feel like the most painful hours of my life. I have to tell myself not to drive like a lunatic in order to get home to Paris faster. I'm so fucking desperate for him, I'm hard as steel as I drive home.

As soon as I step in the door Paris is jumping into my arms and kissing me. I nearly drop him because I'm so unprepared, but I grip his ass cheeks, which are bare, minus two thin straps under his buttocks, and hold him to me. I don't even get the chance to admire whatever it is he's wearing, but I can't stop kissing him back as I carry him to the sofa. Fuck, his kisses are addictive.

"I need you," he whimpers, and I'm realizing just how insatiable my princess is. I lower him onto the couch on his back between kisses, pausing momentarily to strip off my coat and shoes, and then gazing at him as he stares up at me, his face flushed and his gaze heated. My gaze rakes over his body and I slide my hand along his torso, my dick jerking at the sight of him in a lacy black bra and a matching jockstrap. Fuck, he's sexy. His dick is tenting his jock and there's already a wet spot there that has my mouth watering. And something about seeing him in a bra is really doing it for me. Plus that fucking belly button ring. It's a heart this time and it's making my dick throb.

"Damn, you look good," I murmur, before I lean over him and press my lips to his again. We make out for several more seconds and I start to undress while we do. Pretty soon I'm down to my briefs and I'm lavishing his gorgeous body in kisses, licks, and nibbles. I use my finger to play with his nipples while I lick and suck on his belly button, tugging on his ring while I do, and he mewls. Then I press kisses to his straining cock and along his balls, before I move my mouth up, shoving his bra aside, and take his nipple into my mouth. He keens, and his hips arch off the couch. A moan leaves him when I grip his hair and tug.

"Oh, fuck, Chris," he whines. "Please. I need . . ."

"What do you want, baby?" I ask him.

"Eat me. Please? God, I want your mouth on me so bad."

"Fuck," I growl, then press more kisses to his heated skin. "I'm gonna do just that, and then you're gonna ride me until you're spraying all over me, okay?"

His eyes heat and his dick jumps. He nods eagerly and I slide his jock off, tossing it to the floor. I press a few kisses to his bare, leaking cock and then to his heavy balls before I shove a couch pillow under his ass and he gifts me with a perfect view of his pucker. "Goddamn. So fucking pretty." His dick jerks at my words, and I slip my finger down to play with his entrance. He whimpers. "You want me to taste this?" I ask. "You want my mouth on your perfect pretty boy hole?"

"Chris," he whines, his body trembling.

"Keep those legs spread for me, baby," I rasp. Then I bury my face between his cheeks, breathing him in, moaning at the scent of him before my tongue darts out and I lick his pucker.

It flutters wildly for me with every swipe of my tongue and I can't get enough. Not when he's writhing and gasping the way he is. I lick and suck and nibble until my jaw is sore and aching, and then I break for a second to suck his balls into my mouth and he wails. My tongue laves along his sack and then up to his shaft where I slowly lick to the head of his leaking cock and then suckle it for a few seconds as he moans and gasps. He's wrecked, and I love it.

I play with his hard nipples as I suck the head of his dick, sliding my tongue into his slit again and again and feeling him writhe underneath me, gasping my name again and again. Then I make my way back down to his hole. I flutter the tip of my tongue against his entrance for several seconds, and when he sounds like he's about to combust from the pleasure, I slip my tongue inside him.

"Fuck, oh fuck," he wails. "Chris, baby."

God, I want him to come like this. I want to feel his hole clenching around my tongue.

"Shit, Chris, I can't. I'm gonna come," he nearly sobs. "Fuck, baby."

Even if he can't get it up again, which I'm guessing he can, I want this too badly to stop. I reach up blindly for his nipple again and when I find it I pinch, and then tug, and that breaks him. He screams, and I feel his cum on my arm as he shoots, his ass clenching around my tongue so perfectly it makes me almost spill in my briefs.

"Oh, fuck," he breathes. "Oh fuck."

I slide my tongue out of him and stare at him as I wipe the saliva from my chin. He's beautiful, complete and utter rapture on his face.

"God, that was amazing," he mumbles. "I didn't expect to come from that." He pulls me to him and kisses me.

"Still want me to ride you?" he asks.

"If you're up for it."

"One hundred percent," he says, grinning. "I want that dick inside me one way or another."

I grin back and lean forward to lap up his seed. He moans as I slot my lips over his and feed him his own spunk. "Get naked," he says. "I wanna blow you."

I slip my underwear off and toss them aside. He licks his lips as he lowers himself to his knees in front of me. Fuck, that's hot.

"I've never done this before," he says, his cheeks flushing as he leans in and licks the tip of my dick through my piercing, and then takes the piercing between his teeth and tugs gently. I suck in a breath at the sensation and more precum oozes out of the tip as he swirls his tongue around it, sliding it under and around my piercing. He moans when my precum hits his tongue and his eyes flutter closed.

"I think you'll be just fine," I rasp. God, I can't believe he's on his knees for me, and he's already driving me insane with that mouth of his. When he pulls off, my Prince Albert piercing glistens in the low light, precum dripping off of it, mixed with his saliva.

He grips my shaft in his small hand and starts to press kisses to my cock, making me groan and gasp in equal measure. More precum leaks out and my breaths are heavy as he nuzzles my balls and inhales.

"Fuck," I curse, and my dick jerks.

He hums before swiping his tongue slowly along the length of my shaft and then dipping his tongue into my slit.

I cry out, and my hand grips his hair as my head falls back against the couch. Fuck, this is good. He's so eager, so confident. He takes me into his mouth and I groan as my eyes close. He grips the base of my cock in one hand and uses the other to massage my balls, and fuck, it feels good.

"Jesus, Pip," I breathe. I gasp when he takes me deeper, and I force myself to open my eyes so I can see him at work. His head bobs up and down like he was fucking born to suck dick, his cheeks hollowed, and when he looks up at me through long eyelashes, his eyes are lust drunk. Spit coats my dick and slides down his chin.

"God, you look good like this," I tell him, and he flushes, then takes me deeper. I have to work extra hard not to fuck his face. I don't think he's ready for that and I would probably come, which I don't want. But god, his mouth is incredible. So warm and so wet.

"Fuck, baby, stop, or I'm gonna come," I tell him a second later, gripping his hair and pulling him off me.

His eyes are glazed over and his lips are swollen and puffy. I suck in a breath at how hard he is, his cock leaking obscenely.

"Get up here," I order.

He scrambles off the floor and I lie on my back as he straddles me. Holy fuck, the skin on skin contact is almost enough to make me combust. Shit, he's naked, except for the sexy lace bra he's still wearing, and he's on top of me. Holy fuck.

"Oh, god," he moans, and starts rutting against me, his dick moving against mine in a way that has my body singing with pleasure.

"Fuck, baby," I groan. "I need to be inside you."

He nods, but then I realize, "We need lube and a condom. They're in my wallet."

He scrambles off me and locates the necessary items, then climbs back on top of me. He tears the lube open and gets some on his fingers, then reaches back and starts to stretch himself as I slide on the condom.

When the condom is on he slicks my cock up with more lube, and then positions himself. I grip my rock hard dick and he slowly lowers himself onto it. "It's okay, take your time," I tell him, rubbing his belly and stroking his thigh as he takes me in.

He lets out a few deep breaths as I slowly sink inside his tight channel, but then he's impaled on me completely and we're both letting out blissful moans.

"Oh, god. Fuck, that's good. You feel incredible," he says, his hands resting on my chest, his forehead pressed to mine. His body shudders and I kiss him.

"So do you," I rasp. "I love you so fucking much, Pip. Now, ride my cock like you fucking mean it, baby."

He kisses me and then raises himself on my shaft and lowers back down. I groan and so does he. He repeats the motion, his eyes closing and his mouth parting in bliss as he fucks himself on my cock, chasing his release. It's the most incredible thing I've ever seen.

"Fuck, baby, that's it," I encourage. "You look so damn good on top of me. Your ass is so perfect, sweetheart."

He whines and his dick jerks, precum leaking down his shaft and onto my belly. I grip his dick and start to stroke him while he fucks himself, and he slams his mouth against mine, his hips moving at a frantic pace, his tongue tangling with mine.

"Fuck, Pip, I'm so close," I growl. "Give me your tits, baby." He moves his upper body closer to my mouth and I suck and lick on his nipple as I jack him and he rides me, my hips thrusting to meet his as my other hand grips his ass and squeezes. I slide that hand between his cheeks and circle his hole, and he explodes, crying out as his release spills across my chest.

"Fuck, baby," I growl. "I'm gonna come. You make me so damn hard."

He kisses me, and then to my surprise he pulls off me, but I don't have time to worry about it before he's lying back on the couch and saying, "Come on me. I wanna wear your spunk."

I pull off the condom and lean over him, jacking myself hard and fast as I stare at him. "Tell me you love me," I say.

"I love you," he says. "I love you so damn much. And I wanna wear your seed. Cover me in it, baby."

It's so sincere that I blow my load right then and there, my dick pulsing and my cum shooting out all over his small body, his stomach, chest, and even his face. I groan at the sight and his dick gives a twitch.

"Feed it to me?" he says, lying underneath me, looking

debauched and utterly sinful. His bra is soaked in my cum and it's so fucking sexy. I scoop some of it up and bring my finger to his lips. His tongue darts out and he licks it up greedily, moaning at the taste. I swipe up more with my tongue and then feed it to him, and we kiss for a while, tasting me.

"Shower," he says, and I chuckle.

"Did you see stars?" I ask him with a grin.

He grins back. "Baby, I saw the whole damn galaxy."

NINETEEN

CHRIS

We fuck like rabbits over the next week, and I love every second of it. Some of our sex is fast and dirty, but if we can, we take our time. We've fucked on the kitchen table, in the shower, in both our beds, and on the couch mulitple times. And though I've taken him from behind a couple of times, I prefer not to. I love seeing his face, having access to his body, watching him, making eye contact. I love worshipping him and how his body responds to me. I love caring for him. I love making him feel good. And my little princess can't seem to get enough of my dick, or my tongue.

My biggest regret is that we don't have nearly enough time together. We still manage to make love at least once a day for the most part, but we don't get to spend a lot of time together in general. We sometimes have dinner or breakfast together, sometimes not, and usually, if I'm not heading to class or work, I'm shutting myself in my room to do home-work afterwards. He tried keeping me company while I stud-ied, but I was so distracted just by his presence, I had to ask him to leave. I've even had to force myself to go study at the library so I wouldn't have to worry about it.

He's so sweet, though, and he knows I'm stressed and overwhelmed, so he never says anything, doesn't get upset, or hurt, just tells me he loves me and makes his own plans. He has come down to *Spill the Beans* a few times to do his homework and I've been able to talk to him on my breaks, which has honestly meant a lot to me, because as much as I love sex with him, I just want to see him, too.

I want to give him so much more, and maybe after I graduate things will calm down for a bit and I can focus on him the way I want to. The way he deserves. I just have to hope he loves me enough to be patient with me. I'm so crazy about him I don't know what I would do if he decided I wasn't worth it.

The way he looks at me, though, the way he smiles at me, the way he touches me, tells me he won't give up on me so easily. That he wants me to be a part of his life even when things are crazy and stressful.

Tonight is our first actual night out together since we started dating. We've had a few nights in, sex and then a movie type of thing, which I'm not complaining about at all. I actually prefer it most nights because I'm not a huge people person and I'm usually so exhausted that going out doesn't appeal to me, but tonight is the talent show the LBGTQ club is putting on at the student center and Paris and I are going together. I'm actually really looking forward to it. We need this, and I know he's excited to share it with me. My biggest concern is that I'm not sure how we're supposed to act with each other. Do we hold hands? Or is that a bad idea because Preston and Jackson might find out? I have no idea how many people they know who might be there, or if they will be there.

Fuck, maybe it would be easier to just tell them. I hate hiding. I love Paris and I don't want to keep him a secret. But it has only been two weeks and I'm still unsure about how Preston would react, and I don't want to have to deal with that yet.

Since Paris invited me he's driving, and as we make our way there I ask him how he wants to handle things. If he's worried about Preston finding out if we're affectionate with each other.

He grimaces. "God, I want so bad to just hold your hand, or let you put your arm around me, or kiss me. I just…"

I squeeze his thigh. "It's okay. I get it. We can be chill tonight. It's not ideal, but I understand. I'm not really sure the best way to handle this either."

He gives me a soft smile. "Thank you. I'm really glad you're here."

It turns out Jackson and Preston and Rory and Parker are at the talent show, supporting some of their friends that are performing, so Paris and I keep our hands to ourselves like we planned, which is much more difficult than I anticipated. I have to stop myself from reaching for him several times throughout the evening, and if the way he's looking at me is anything to go by, so is he.

The talent show is amazing though. There's singing, dancing, some short skits, multiple people playing different musical instruments including guitar, piano, violin, and flute. There's a comedian that is actually pretty funny, a couple of drag performers that have amazing outfits and do a fantastic job lip synching, some magic tricks, a couple who do some super impressive juggling acts, and more. I'm honestly blown away by the level of talent and can't stop smiling.

We meet up with our friends after the show, and when they invite us to go out for dinner we accept. But I will tell you, it sucks to be in a relationship, to be in love with someone and to feel like you have to hide it from your closest friends. Maybe we're being too cautious. Maybe Preston wouldn't care. He's a pretty chill person. And even if he did care, it wouldn't change how I felt about Paris. He'd have to get over it eventually.

At least we have the car ride to be affectionate with each other, and we don't waste it. We're touching each other in little ways the entire drive, and I'm so distracted, and so damn turned on, I don't realize we've turned into the wrong parking lot until Paris parks the car. I look around me at the abandoned building and the empty space.

"What are we–" I start, but don't get to finish before Paris is in my lap, gripping my face and sucking on my tongue. He whimpers as he ruts against me.

Fuck. I kiss him back, my cock pressing painfully against my zipper. "Fuck, baby," I breathe when he finally lets me come up for air. "We'll be late."

"Shut up and get your cock out," he orders as he shoves his coat off and unbuttons his jeans. And okay, I think I like this bossy side of him. And I'll admit, the idea of getting frisky with him in a deserted parking lot is really doing it for me.

I unbutton and unzip my jeans, then shove my own coat aside, before I lower my briefs just enough to let my cock spring free. It's hard and leaking, and I suck in a breath when I see that his is the same. He presses his body against mine and murmurs against my lips, "Jerk us off, baby."

I hold my hand under his mouth and he spits in my palm. It's not a lot but mixed with our precum it'll do. I grip us both and start to stroke, and my eyes roll back in my head at the sensation. God, it's incredible.

"Fuck, you feel so good," he whines, peppering my face and neck with kisses. "Fuck, baby."

"Jesus, Pip, you're driving me insane," I rasp out as his hand finds its way under my shirt and he tweaks my nipple. My head falls back against the seat as he lavishes me with more kisses and I stroke us faster.

"Love your cock, baby," he murmurs. "God you smell amazing."

I grip his hair in my other hand and tug and he shivers as he sucks on my neck. "Fuck, princess, I'm gonna come."

"Me, too."

I grip his hair tighter and lift his head so our eyes are

locked. Despite the darkness I can see that his pupils are blown and his lips are puffy. "Kiss me," I tell him, and then slam my mouth against his.

He whimpers and then we kiss fiercely as I jack us together, our cocks slick with all the precum that's gathered. Just the thought of our juices mingling has a flare of desire and possessiveness racing through me and I suck harder on Paris's tongue. "Mine," I hear myself growl. "Fuck, this gorgeous cock is mine."

"Yes," he pants. "Fuck, yes, it's yours. It's all yours, baby. All of me is yours."

That's all it takes for me to shoot my load all over my hand and both of our cocks, and my dick bucks when I feel his cock spasming and releasing against mine. Fuck, that's hot as hell. My hand is soaked, and there's spunk on Paris's bare abdomen under the cropped sweater he's wearing.

Fuck, a small amount got on my shirt, too. But I'll just leave my coat on during dinner and hopefully no one will be the wiser.

Speaking of dinner. "We need to go," I say.

He grips my hand and brings it to his mouth before licking it clean. God, I'll never get tired of seeing him swallow our spunk. I kiss him again, and then he scrambles back into his own seat. I grab the wipes from the glove compartment and hand him a couple as I work on cleaning the rest of the mess off myself. It's not until we're back on the road that I realize I have two missed texts from Preston asking if every-thing is okay and if we're still coming.

When we arrive at the restaurant we're about fifteen minutes late. Jackson raises an eyebrow at us when we take our seats.

"What happened?" Preston asks, and the concern in his voice actually has me feeling a little guilty. *Well, best friend, I was banging your little brother in an abandoned parking lot.* Somehow I don't feel like that would go over so great.

"Took a wrong turn," Paris says.

"A wrong turn?" Parker asks, looking at me. "In the town you've lived in for three years?" Rory not so subtly jabs his fiancé in the ribs with his elbow.

"Ow, freckles, what was that for?" Parker asks, his voice so innocent it hurts a little.

"I'm not great at driving in the dark," Paris lies. "My bad."

"You gonna take your coat off?" Preston asks me.

"No, I'm kinda cold," I lie. That earns me another look from Jackson and I try not to squirm.

"Okay," Preston says, drawing the word out. "Well, they should be back any second. We told them we were waiting on you guys."

"So, you excited for the play?" I ask Jackson, trying desperately to change the subject. "Next week, right?"

Jackson nods. "Opening night is Thursday."

"He's gonna be amazing," Preston says, then kisses his boyfriend on the cheek. Jackson blushes, which isn't something I've seen him do much. It's sweet how much Preston flusters him.

"We're super excited," Rory pipes up. "We have great seats, too. I've never seen *West Side Story*."

I gape at him. "Seriously?"

He shakes his head. "I don't want to know. I don't want any spoilers before the play."

"So, how are everyone's classes going?" Parker asks after the waiter returns to take our orders and scurries off again. We all groan but take turns sharing. Rory is an art major, which I'm super impressed by. I've seen his work and it's amazing. Jackson, of course, is a theater major. Parker is majoring in Phys Ed and wants to be a physical education teacher, which I think he'd be great at since he's so good with kids. Preston is pre-med and wants to be an endocrinologist, so we've both got quite a few more years of schooling ahead of us, but I like that we have some classes together or I'd see him even less and it's another thing we have in common.

Paris shares how his gen ed and psych classes are going. Preston smiles the whole time Paris is talking and it warms my insides. He always told me how talented and smart Paris is, and it was never with any sort of jealousy or insecurity. I mean, Preston is bright, too, but Paris is one of those people that seems to be exceptional at everything they set their minds to, and he's a super fast learner. He's also got a lot of heart and a tender spirit, which is one of the reasons I love him so much, and why I know he'll be an amazing therapist for the queer community.

The talk turns to what everyone's plans are for Thanksgiving since it's only a couple of weeks away, and that's when I realize I'll be going home for Thanksgiving with Paris, Preston, and Jackson, and there's no fucking way I can keep from being affectionate with Paris the entire time I'm there. His hand brushes my leg under the table and I wonder if he's thinking the same thing.

We might have to tell Preston sooner rather than later whether we like it or not.

TWENTY

CHRIS

It's opening night of *West Side Story* and Paris and I are getting ready to meet Preston in the lobby of the school theater in about an hour. We're getting ready in our own rooms, nothing fancy, but I don't want to wear the same clothes I wore to classes. I had to make sure I had tonight off from the cafe so I could make it, and despite how exhausted I am, I'm honestly excited to see the show. I love performance art, and of course I love spending time with Preston.

The worst part, once again, will be being with Paris and not being able to touch him the way I want to. We talked about it, and decided we'd tell Preston and Jackson about us over Thanksgiving break. That gives us a little bit more time to prepare ourselves.

I'm standing in front of the bathroom mirror, washing my face and hoping I can get the nausea that's settled in my stomach to abate. I've been feeling a little off all day but I know if I can get a decent night's rest after the play I'll be fine.

I'm drying my face and hands when a wave of dizziness hits me, and then my vision starts to tunnel as my heart rate drops.

The last thing I remember is wishing I was standing over carpet.

PARIS

I haven't been this excited about an event in a long time. I can't actually remember the last time I saw a play and I love West Side Story. Musicals in general are amazing. I love the singing, the costumes, but I think my favorite part is the dancing.

I make the final touches to my makeup and then give myself one last look in the mirror, before turning off the light and heading into the living room. Since it generally takes me a while longer to get ready I expect Chris to already be waiting for me, but he's not in the living room. He's not in the kitchen, so I head back to his bedroom to see if he got held up or needs any help. He's not there either, so I figure he's in the bathroom, but there's no sound coming from that direction. No running water, or the sound of him brushing his teeth, or a toilet flushing.

"Chris?" I say, walking towards the partially open bathroom door. "Baby?" I knock just in case, but when there's no answer I push the door open. My heart stops and my stomach bottoms out when I see Chris passed out on the bathroom floor.

"Oh my god," I cry, rushing to his side as tears spill down my cheeks. "Baby," I roll him onto his back and tap his face, and to my relief his eyes slowly start to flutter open.

"Oh my god," I cry again, gripping his face in my hands as I sob and hold him to me.

"Pip?" he groans, his voice weak. "What happened?" He slowly starts to sit up but he looks pained as he does, his eyes squinting and a hand on his head. His skin is clammy and paler than normal as he rests his head against the bathroom wall.

"You passed out," I tell him, trying to gain control of

myself. But fuck, the man I love was unconscious on the floor. My heart is still racing. "I should call an ambulance," I add and take out my phone. His hand is on mine before I can dial. I look at him and he shakes his head, then winces.

"No," he grunts out. "No ambulance. I'm fine."

I gape at him. "You were unconscious. And I don't even know for how long. You need to go to the hospital."

"No," he says again, more firmly. "I don't."

"Chris." I can't believe he's being stubborn right now. "You might have a concussion and we have no idea why you passed out. This could be serious."

"I'm fine," he says, and I want to fucking scream. There's no blood anywhere, which is good, but I know serious injuries don't always involve blood. "I just need a minute."

I bite my lip. I hate this. I know he needs a doctor. He is far from fine and I'm scared out of my mind. But what can I do? I can't make him go.

After a few minutes of just sitting there feeling like I should be doing something I say, "We should get you to bed. Are you up for standing?" He nods and I get to my feet before helping him up.

"I'll just lay down for a few minutes and then we can leave," he says, and I nearly feel steam coming out of my ears. I wait until he's on his bed before I respond.

"You are not going anywhere tonight. You look like shit."

"I'm okay, Pip," he says, gripping my hand in his and looking at me. "I just got a little lightheaded. It's okay. I'm okay. I want to go."

Goddamn it. "I'm worried about you."

"I know, but you don't need to be. I'm okay." I know he wants to believe that, but the evidence suggests otherwise. He's overworked, exhausted, stressed, and overwhelmed. And I'm pretty sure the reason he doesn't want to go to a doctor is because he doesn't want to spend the money. That, or he can't have them telling him to take it easy. As long as he doesn't see a doctor, he can go on telling himself he's fine.

Fuck. "You want some water or juice or something?" I ask. He kisses my hand and it softens a little bit of my anger, but does nothing to lessen my worry.

"Sure."

I go to the kitchen and grab a bottle of Gatorade and bring it back to him. It might not help at all, but I need to feel like I'm doing something. He sits and drinks it slowly then sets it on his nightstand. His color is better than it was a few minutes ago and his skin feels more normal when I touch his forehead. I run my fingers through his short curls. "How are you feeling?"

"Better," he says, and gives me a small smile.

"Does your head hurt?"

"A little, but not too much."

"I should drive tonight, to be on the safe side. And you're going to tell me if you start to not feel well. Promise."

He squeezes my hand and even though I know it's hard for him, he nods.

I still think we should cancel, but again, I can't make him stay, and if he is insisting on going I'm going to be there, too.

Of course we have to lie when we get to the theater and Preston asks if everything is okay. I make up a story about how I just couldn't decide what shirt to wear. I desperately want to tell him what happened, but I know Chris would be pissed.

We take our seats, Chris in the middle, only a few minutes before the curtain goes up. I wish I could say I love it, which I do, but I'm honestly so worried about Chris I don't enjoy it nearly as much as I want to.

Chris is okay. He seems like his normal self throughout the show and when we get back to the apartment, but I have to keep myself from clinging to him like saran wrap as we stand in the lobby after the play and shake hands with the actors and congratulate Jackson.

I barely sleep that night, even though he drifts off almost as soon as we're in his bed. I wake him a couple of times in the night to make sure he's okay. He grumbles, but at least I know he's alive and his brain is working.

The next day I try to convince him to take it easy and skip classes and work, and he refuses, saying he can rest the following day when he doesn't have places to be. I insist on driving him to classes and work which means adjusting my schedule a little bit, and he grumbles about that, too, but reluctantly agrees.

"Are you going to tell your parents what happened?" I ask him that night as I drive us back to the apartment after picking him up from *Spill the Beans*. He made it through the day, but I can tell he's even more peaked than normal, and his mood is off. I wouldn't be surprised if he has a headache he's not telling me about.

"I don't want to worry them," he says, staring out the window. "And there's nothing they can do."

I sigh, but I at least convince him to go to bed early that night.

He does seem better in the morning, and after resting for a good portion of the day I'm feeling a bit less worried about him. He agrees to stay off screens as much as possible and not go anywhere. I bring him food and drinks in bed and we do a lot of cuddling, which is honestly really nice.

And we may or may not exchange hand jobs. And maybe a blow job. What can I say, he's bored and I love his dick. Besides, if it helps him relax and get some much needed sleep, why not?

He passed out after I sucked his soul out through his cock, his words not mine. And I have to say I'm feeling pretty good about my oral skills these days. That dick piercing makes it even more fun to suck his cock and he always makes the best noises. It's a heady feeling knowing I make him feel so good.

I snuggle up next to him and drape my arm over his torso before I drift to sleep, listening to his breaths and hearing the steady thump thump of his heart, wishing I knew how to make all his struggles go away.

TWENTY-ONE

PARIS

Leaving now, Chris texts both me and Preston in a group chat. *Should be there in a couple of hours.*

It's three days into Thanksgiving break and I'm home with my family, including Jackson. His parents are shitty assholes who have neglected him his entire life so he's been an honorary member of our family since he and Preston started dating.

Ginger is curled up on my lap, snoring softly. *Star Trek* is on the television because we watch it as a family whenever we can. The house smells like pumpkin and nutmeg. The Christmas decorations are up now. Jackson, Preston, and I helped Dad bring all the boxes up from the basement. The only thing not out is the tree because we're doing that the day after tomorrow so Chris can be here, too.

We spent the day ice skating and then came back home to drink hot chocolate and play games. It's honestly been the perfect day, except for the fact that my boyfriend isn't here. He insisted on staying a few extra days to work before he made the drive. I didn't like the idea, but I knew I wouldn't be able to talk him out of it, and since he's been doing okay since his incident I didn't press the issue. There's a niggling feeling in the back of my head though, that's making me think I should have.

I text him in the group chat. *See you soon.* Then I open our text chain and type *Text me in an hour please. Drive safe. I love you.* He responds with a thumbs up and a kissy face emoji.

God, I love him so much. And being away from him for the past few days has been torture. I need him in my arms, I need his kisses and his touch and his smile. I need him wrapped around me in bed at night.

I need to know he's safe.

"Another episode?" Preston asks once the current episode of Star Trek is over. He and Jackson are curled up on the sofa adjacent to the one I'm on with Ginger. Dad is in his recliner and Mom is in the rocking chair near the wood burning stove.

My phone buzzes just then and I check to see he's an hour out now. "Chris should be here by dinner time," I say, relief filling me.

Preston checks his phone and frowns. "He didn't text that to both of us."

I shrug. "Probably just forgot."

Preston's frown deepens, but he doesn't say anything.

We start another episode of *Star Trek* and by the time it's finished Mom is calling us all to the table.

My leg bounces and I bite my lip as I check my phone repeatedly over the next twenty minutes, because Chris still isn't here.

"What's wrong?" Dad asks after the hundredth time of me looking for a message that I know isn't there.

"Shouldn't he be here by now?" I ask. I probably sound more worried than a person should be over the wellbeing of their roommate, but I don't care.

"It's dark out, and the roads are a little icy. He's probably just being extra careful and taking it slow," Preston assures me, but I can tell he's getting a little nervous, and Jackson reaches over to rub his back.

But when another fifteen minutes goes by I have to text him again. When another ten minutes goes by and there's no reply, and when Preston calls him and it goes to his voicemail, I feel like I'm about to have a panic attack.

Something is very wrong.

"We should go look for him," I say, my stomach churning and my heart in my throat. I have to keep the tears at bay as my body starts to tremble. "Like you said, it's dark, and the roads are icy, and there's not a lot of traffic, and if something happened . . . " I wipe at my cheek as a tear slips free.

My parents exchange worried glances.

"I'll drive," Jackson says, and he, Preston and I leave the table.

"Be safe," Mom says. "Please keep us updated."

When I look at my brother his face is pale. He looks exactly how I feel, and of course he does. Chris is his best friend.

Jackson squeezes his hand, and we bundle up in our winter gear before we head out the door into the winter night.

I'm in the back seat of Preston's car and Jackson is behind the wheel, driving slowly, all of us keeping our eyes peeled. I'm so damn scared, I might puke, and I have to keep wiping tears from my cheeks.

It's been twenty minutes and there's no sign of any accidents, which I guess is a good thing, but then we spot red and blue lights up ahead and I have to keep a scream from tearing through my throat as we get closer and I see multiple police cars, an ambulance, and a firetruck blocking the dirt road.

"Oh my god," I wail, and nearly collapse when I throw myself out of the car before Jackson's even come to a complete stop.

"Shit, Paris," Preston calls after me, but I barely hear him as I run forward. I don't see Chris's car until I'm almost on top of the emergency vehicles and a female cop is telling me to back up. But I don't. I can't. My boyfriend's car is wrapped around a tree, and I can't think, I can't breathe. Then I see a stretcher being wheeled towards the back of a waiting ambulance, and the sight of Chris's body on it has me letting out a strangled sob. He has an oxygen mask on his face and a C-collar, but I can't tell if he's conscious or not. I'm assuming that since he's not in a body bag he's at least alive, which has hope surging through me, and the relief is so profound my knees buckle.

"Chris!" I shout. "Can I see him?" I manage to croak out through the tears. "Please, he's my boyfriend."

The cop's expression softens. "I'm afraid I can't let you through," she tells me. "But you can follow him to the hospital."

I sense movement behind me and then I hear Jackson's voice. "Can you tell us what hospital they're taking him to?"

The cop says something but I'm so lost in my emotions I can't process it. All I see is the man I love being lifted into the back of the ambulance and the doors closing behind him.

He's alive. He's alive. He's alive, is what I keep telling myself as Preston and Jackson help me back to the car.

TWENTY-TWO

PARIS

"You should drink something," Mom says, handing me a cup of water. She and Dad have joined Preston, Jackson, and I in the hospital's ICU waiting room. It feels like it's been hours since we got here and asked about Chris, only to be told they couldn't share medical information with non-family.

I'm curled up in a chair with my arms wrapped around my knees trying not to throw up, and I'm wiping tears from my cheeks every five seconds. I haven't been this scared since Mom and Dad had cancer. Or this sick to my stomach and beside myself since Phoenix died.

I can't lose him. He's my whole world.

Preston is sitting with his head in his hands as Jackson alternates between rubbing his back and carding his fingers through his hair.

We got a hold of Chris's parents. Well, Preston did, and they're on their way, but it'll be another few hours before they can get here, even though they're taking the first flight they can from Minnesota.

I take the cup, but I only manage a couple of sips before I'm setting it aside again.

Mom sits down beside me and tucks my head into her shoulder and I sob. "I know," she says. "I know."

Dad is standing up pacing the area.

After another half an hour and feeling like I'm going to crawl out of my skin I approach the desk again which has a different receptionist than last time. "Can you tell me if there's any update on Christopher Rose?" I ask. "He was in a car accident. I just want to know if he's okay."

"Are you family?" the middle aged white woman asks me, not unkindly.

"No," I admit. "He's my boyfriend."

"Let me get a nurse for you," she says, and I nod, before going back to my seat.

It's another thirty minutes before a nurse approaches us. "Family for Christopher Rose?" she asks and we all look up, then stand.

"I understand you are wondering about Chris's condition after the accident. Are you family?"

"In every way but blood," Preston says, his voice broken. My brother hasn't been this distraught since our brother died, and I can't imagine what would happen to him if he lost his best friend.

"I'm afraid I can't tell you any specific details. But I can tell you that he's stable."

I wobble, and a breath leaves me. Dad grips my arm to keep me upright.

"Will we be able to see him soon?" I ask.

"We're still running tests right now. After that if he's up for visitors and gives his consent it's restricted to visiting hours and only two at a time."

"Thank you," I breathe, tears streaking my cheeks.

She nods and gives a soft smile. "It looks like he has a lot of support, which we always like to see. Hang in there, okay?"

CHRIS

Everything hurts, even on the pain meds they gave me. I feel like I was hit by a Mac truck. My body aches, my neck is stiff and sore, my head is throbbing, I feel nauseated and dizzy thanks to the concussion they told me I have, and my left wrist is broken, so it's in a splint.

But my chest is the worst. Every breath is painful and they tell me I have a few broken ribs and a collapsed lung. There's a pulse oximeter on my finger and a blood pressure cuff on my upper arm. An IV is in my right hand, a nasal cannula in my nose, and the incessant beeping of the machines to my side. I also have a chest tube due to the collapsed lung. And of course I'm dressed in one of their stupid hospital gowns.

I'm kind of freaking out, if I'm being honest. I know I fucked up big time. I fell asleep behind the wheel, and from what the doctor tells me, I'm lucky that my injuries aren't worse.

"Your heart looks good, liver and kidneys are good, but your blood work does show some elevated cortisol and your vitamin B12 levels are low. Nothing particularly alarming or abnormal about that given your age, but I would recommend you follow up with a GP when you discharge," the doctor, a middle aged white woman with fair skin and dark eyes tells me as she looks through the papers on her chart. She pauses and looks at me. "Right now the most important thing you can do is rest. You'll be here until the chest tube can be removed, at which point you'll be transferred to a lesser unit for monitoring."

She asks if I have any questions, and when I say I don't, she leaves, the door closing with a click behind her.

A second later there's a knock on the door and then it slowly opens. Paris appears looking disheveled and exhausted, his hair a mess, and his eyes red and puffy. The look on his face tells me I look just as bad as I feel. But god, he's here.

"Hey, Pip," I rasp.

His bottom lip quivers and then he's by my side as tears streak his cheeks.

"I'm so sorry," I say as he grips my face gently, and tears start to slide down my cheeks, too. And let me tell you, crying with broken ribs is not fun.

He shakes his head. "You're alive, you're here. That's all that matters." He presses a kiss to my head and something inside me loosens. I honestly think I was afraid he'd be pissed at me. That he might even break up with me because I've been so damn stubborn and irresponsible. "I fucked up," I tell him as more tears fall. "I should have listened to you."

He presses a finger to my lips. "Stop. Not now, okay? You need rest. I don't want you feeling guilty. That won't help you. You're going to be okay, and we're going to figure this out. I promise."

I nod. "I'm really glad you're here."

"Me, too. My parents are in the waiting area. So are Jackson and Preston."

I swallow. "Preston. Does he know?"

"I'm guessing he does after the way I've been acting since you got hurt. I also told the police officer and the receptionist I was your boyfriend and I don't know if he overheard, but I was past caring at that point. We haven't talked about it yet. He's pretty freaked out, though. I think he'd like to see you."

I nod again, and he kisses my hand. "I'll let him come say hi and then I'm planning to be here for as long as the staff will let me. And we called your parents. They should be here soon."

I give him a small smile and he disappears. God, my parents. My mom, flying all the way here because of me when it's so difficult for her to travel. The cost of flights, of being in this hospital, of the fucking ambulance ride, the car being totalled, everything. Here I was pushing myself to try and help them and I made it so much worse instead.

I sigh and rest my head back just as there's another knock

on the door, and then Preston peeks his head inside. He looks more upset than I've ever seen him, not angry but distressed, and he wipes tears from his eyes as he closes the door behind him.

"Hey, asshole," he jibes, and I chuckle. I know he's struggling and trying to lighten the mood. But more tears slide down his cheeks as he sits in the chair beside me. "Fuck, you scared the shit out of me, man. Are you okay?"

"More or less," I say. "I'm gonna be here for a bit it sounds like, and I think I'm gonna be making some life adjustments, but yeah, I'm okay. Physically anyway."

He nods as he wipes his tears and runs his fingers through his blond hair. "What happened?" he asks.

I swallow and tell him everything. Well, I don't say anything about Paris and me. I don't think now is the time, but I tell him about how he was right. How I've been pushing myself, and pushing myself, and how depleted I've been, how exhausted and stressed and overwhelmed. I tell him that I passed out the night of Jackson's play and his eyes go wide. Then I tell him I fell asleep behind the wheel because I was so damn tired. "I'm not okay," I admit. "I'm not." More tears fall from my eyes and he squeezes my arm.

"You're going to be," he tells me. "You are going to rest and recuperate and we're going to figure things out once you get out of here. You know I'm here for you, no matter what."

"Yeah, thanks."

There's another knock on the door and when it opens my parents are there. "You must be Mr. and Mrs. Rose," Preston says, standing to shake their hands. "I'm Preston."

"It's so nice to finally meet you, Preston," Mom says with a soft smile on her face. "I'm so glad Chris has a friend like you. We just met your family and they are lovely. We're so grateful you've taken care of our boy."

"Of course. Chris is family. I'll give you some privacy," Preston says. He nudges my shoulder gently. "See you tomorrow."

Mom leans over and presses a soft kiss to my forehead once he's gone, and Dad removes his glasses to wipe tears from his eyes. He's always been a softy.

"How are you feeling?" Mom asks.

"Like shit," I admit.

"You know," she says, sitting on the side of the bed and stroking my cheek, her eyes warm and soft. "When I imagined my children following in my footsteps, trips to the hospital weren't what I had in mind."

"I'm so sorry, Mom," I blubber. God, I'm doing a lot of apologizing.

"What on earth are you sorry for?" she asks, and when I look at Dad his brows are furrowed.

"For making you come out here. For how much money this is going to cost. For fucking up so badly. For failing."

"Christopher Anthony Rose, what in the world have you failed at?"

"I wanted to help you guys," I say. "I wanted to make things easier for you."

"What do you mean?" Dad asks, exchanging a look with Mom. So I do more confessing. I tell them how I've been working way more than we agreed on so I could afford things on my own, so I wouldn't need their help. So I can pay for grad school, and take care of my living expenses, and how I wanted to pay them back eventually for everything because I know they're struggling and I don't want Mom going without her meds or her treatment. I tell them the same things I told Preston about passing out and about falling asleep at the wheel. And by the time I'm finished I'm beyond exhausted.

They don't get angry. They aren't scowling at me. They don't look disappointed. Just concerned. "You need to rest right now," Mom says. "We can talk more later, okay?"

I nod. She kisses my forehead again. "Get some sleep. I'm glad you're okay."

Dad leans over and presses a kiss to the same spot Mom did. "We love you, more than anything," he tells me.

TWENTY-THREE

PARIS

"Hey," I hear, and look up from my spot in the hospital cafeteria where I'm sipping on a coffee and eating a subpar turkey sandwich. Chris is resting now. Mom and Dad and Chris's parents are back at the house trying to rest themselves. And I have no idea where Jackson is, but I'm assuming he's around somewhere because he wouldn't go far from my brother's side right now.

Preston stands over me, hands in his pockets, looking exhausted and a bit nervous. His purple ball cap is on his head and his eyes don't quite meet mine.

"Hey," I reply. "How are you doing?"

He shrugs and lets out a breath. "Okay, I guess." He clears his throat. "I uh, I thought maybe we should talk."

I nod. "Yeah, I guess so."

He sits and takes his hat off, running his fingers through his hair before he puts the hat back on. His forearms rest on the small table between us and he picks at his fingernails. "So you and Chris are . . . " he starts.

"In love," I say. I'm not going to sugar coat it or downplay it. We're not just together, or dating, or seeing each other. I'm in love with him, and if that's hard for my brother to hear then it is.

He nods, but doesn't say anything for several moments. Then, his eyes still downcast he says, "How long?"

"Um, not very, actually. I mean, I've been in love with him for a while. Pretty much since the first day, but he was so obsessed with you he never–" I cut myself off and slap a hand over my mouth. Shit. That wasn't supposed to come out.

Preston's gaze snaps to mine, his eyes wide and his face flushed. "What?"

Shit, shit, shit! Me and my big mouth. "Nothing," I try to backpedal, shaking my head.

He swallows, his flush deepening. "What do you mean he was obsessed with me?"

"I shouldn't have said anything," I say. "But if you want to know more you'll have to ask him. It's not my place." Goddamn it, I hope Chris doesn't hate me for this.

He looks beyond flustered and confused but he nods. "You've been in love with him from the first day?"

I nod. "I mean, that's probably a bit of an exaggeration, but yeah, pretty close. He didn't start having feelings for me until we moved in together. And we've only been officially together for a few weeks. It's really new. That's why we didn't tell you. We weren't sure how you would respond and we needed time. We planned to tell you over break, and then . . ." I trail off. "Are you mad?"

He takes a deep breath and lets it out. "I don't think so. I mean, if anything I'm more mad at myself than you guys. I feel like I'm just clueless when it comes to this stuff. And thinking back it makes sense, the way you guys acted around each other. I'm pretty sure Jackson knew something was up. Hell, I'm pretty sure Rory and Parker knew, but I didn't. How am I so dense?"

I chuckle at that, and my body relaxes. Honestly I wasn't sure how he'd feel about me being with his best friend, or his best friend being with me, and I told myself it didn't matter, that nothing could tear me away from Chris, but it still would have hurt and sucked gummy bears if he'd been upset. His support isn't necessary, but it means a lot and makes things so much easier. "Maybe it just never occurred to you as a possibility."

"Maybe," he says. "But maybe it should have. You're both so amazing and I honestly can't think of anyone else I'd approve of you being with. Not that you need my approval, but . . ."

I smile. "I know what you mean. You're my big brother, it's in your nature to look after me."

He gives a crooked smile, and I know we're going to be okay. Better than okay. "You happy?"

My smile widens and my cheeks heat. "Very happy. I worry about him, and I just hope he's really going to be okay after all this, but I'm not going anywhere, no matter what. I love him with all that I am."

CHRIS

It's been twenty-four hours and my body still hurts all over. Not surprising. I'm not getting a ton of sleep, partially because of the pain, but also because it's a hospital, so every twenty minutes doctors and nurses and janitors and support staff are coming in to talk to me, or clean my room, or deliver meals, or administer meds, or do neurological checks because of the concussion, or my blood pressure cuff is going off and squeezing the bejeezus out of my arm.

And the worst part is trying to eat with one wrist out of commission and my chest feeling like an elephant is sitting on it, and the fact that when I'm awake I can't be on screens so I'm bored out of my mind. The only thing I do have is my music since miraculously my phone made it through the crash. I'm on pain meds, but they aren't making me so loopy I can't function and I need something to do.

So I've had my favorite ladies on repeat and honestly it's

helping some with my stress level, which is pretty high. The pain is distracting me somewhat from thinking about how much work I will miss because of this, how hard it will be to get to classes, and the fact that I no longer have a car. God, I've been working so hard to keep my scholarship, pushing myself even more since I had that talk with my professor, and what if I still lose it because of this? What if my grades suffer?

I take a breath, which is acutely painful, and let it out, trying to calm my nervous system, because I'm realizing more and more it's something I really need to work on. I've thought a little bit about talking to a therapist, but I don't think it's something I'm ready for quite yet. The nurse recommended yoga as a way to help relieve stress, along with meditation, and exercise, once I'm feeling better. But I think I need more than that. I just have to work on being okay with getting help. I've been telling myself for so long that I'm fine, that I can handle it, that I've got it under control, and I'm coming to grips with how untrue that is. I honestly don't know how to not be stressed about my parents though, or to try and make things easier or better for them. I don't know how to not be worried about the things I'm worried about and want to fix it.

A knock on the door pulls me out of my thoughts and I welcome the distraction. I smile when Preston enters and closes the door behind him, but it falters a little when I see him biting his lip. He looks stiff and awkward.

"Hey," I say. "You okay?"

He chuckles as he walks closer. "I should be asking you that." He takes a seat in the chair next to me, but he has trouble meeting my eyes. He rubs the back of his neck with his hand. I get the impression he wants to say something but isn't sure how.

"Is this about Paris?" I ask. "If you're pissed at me just get it out, but you should know I'm crazy about him, and while I want your blessing I don't need it."

He does meet my gaze then, and to my surprise he's smiling. "Yeah, I just talked to him a bit ago about the two of you.

I'm not pissed. Just processing it all, I guess. But honestly, if my baby brother is going to be in love with someone, I can't imagine anyone better than you."

I take a breath and let it out. "Thank you. Though I'm not sure I deserve him."

"Of course you do. You're the best guy I know. And he makes you happy. You deserve to be happy."

To my surprise a tear slides down my cheek.

Preston looks away again and clears his throat.

"Is there something else?" I ask, wondering what else there could be.

He rubs his palms on his jeans and then blurts, "Were you in love with me?"

My face feels like it's on fire and my body starts to tremble as my stomach knots. When I don't immediately deny it Preston's eyes widen. "Fuck," he says.

"It's not a big deal," I reply, trying to keep my voice steady.

"Oh my god." He buries his face in his hands. "Fuck, I was so damn clueless, Chris. This whole time. And I was asking you to help me hook up with other guys, talking non-stop about Jackson." His eyes widen even more. "Oh my god, I had you help me set up a Grindr profile. Fuck, I'm such an asshole."

I can't help it, that makes me laugh. "You're not an asshole. And how could you have known when I never said anything?"

"Why didn't you?"

I chuckle again and then wince at the pain. "You were straight, and then you had your heart set on Jackson. I wasn't going to ruin that with my feelings. I wanted you to be happy. I'd never seen you happier than when you were with him."

He grins. "This is why I know my brother couldn't find anyone better. Because you are just a damn good person, Chris. The best person."

"I don't know about that," I admit. "I love him so much,

but sometimes I feel like I'm just causing him more problems."

He frowns. "Why? Because you're stressed? Because your life isn't rainbows and butterflies? You don't have to have all your shit together and have zero issues to be loveable or make someone else's life better. We all have things we need to work on, we all have hardships. But the right person isn't going to run from those things. They're going to support you and help you. And that's what Paris wants to do because he loves you. I know my little brother, and he spent a lot of his life feeling like he had to pretend, to fit inside a box, to make himself smaller in order to fit in and make other people more comfortable. And I know you help him shine. You see him, Chris. You bring out the best in him. If I wasn't so blind I'd have seen how perfect you two were for each other a long time ago."

I'm not sure how to respond, so I don't. But I'm suddenly aching to see my boyfriend. "Can you ask him to come see me?"

Preston smiles. "Yeah, of course. There's nowhere else he'd rather be."

TWENTY-FOUR

CHRIS

"How's my baby boy?" Mom asks as she sits down next to me and takes my hand. I haven't seen her or Dad since they visited me yesterday. I figured she'd need time to rest after her trip. She didn't look good when she got here but she seems a little better now. When I texted to ask where they were staying she told me Preston's parents were putting them up, which I am incredibly thankful for. They don't need to be paying for a hotel on top of everything else.

Her dark brown hair is in its usual ponytail and she's wearing leggings and an oversized sweater. She looks tired but she's smiling and her deep brown eyes have their usual sparkle.

"I'm okay," I tell her. "Is Dad here?"

"He's in the waiting area. He thought we could use some time alone." She gives me a soft smile and squeezes my hand.

"I'm assuming you have already thought through the fact that pushing yourself the way you have been isn't sustainable, or wise, and that it could affect your scholarship, and your chances of getting into grad school." She's not upset when she says it, just concerned.

I nod. "I thought I could make it work."

"I know." She sighs. "You know, I've always been a pretty independent person. Self-reliant, capable, self-sufficient. And I always took pride in that. But being chronically ill has taught me a lot, and one of the things it's taught me is that leaning on people, admitting you are struggling, asking for help, saying you can't, and having a support system, are not things to be ashamed of. It's also taught me that this world isn't built for people with disabilities. Especially when those disabilities aren't visible or widely understood. Being in pain or feeling sick all the time is hard, but a lot of the exhaustion comes from just advocating for yourself. It's taught me that life is unpredictable. But most of all, I think it's taught me that when you do reach out and say 'I can't', people reach back. And maybe we're just blessed to have so many amazing people surrounding us, because I'm sure not everyone in our situation has that, but your father and I, we've experienced so much love, support and kindness over the last several years. And yes, there have been struggles. There have been some really hard days, some really hard weeks, even months. And yes, we've had to make sacrifices for our children, but those are sacrifices we are happy to make." She looks into my eyes. "Sacrifices I'm happy to make. Because of all the things I've created, you three are my pride and joy. You are my priceless works of art. You are my heart. And while I get frustrated and sad and I've dealt with a lot of grief over the years about my life not going the way I planned, and all the things I've lost, the only thing that hurts more than that, is the thought of anything happening to my children."

Tears are sliding down my cheeks again. "Mom, I'm sorry."

She shakes her head as tears slide down her cheeks, too. Honestly I can't remember the last time I saw her cry. "No, don't you apologize. You have nothing to be sorry for. If anyone should be apologizing it's your father and I. For not noticing what was going on. I'm sorry you felt like you had to do so much. I love that you have such a big heart, Chris. I love how compassionate you are, how hard working, devoted and caring. I am so proud of you every single day. And I know you wish things were different for me, for our family. I know, baby. I know it's hard. But I can't have you killing yourself trying to fix it. You aren't Superman, and it's not your job to make it better. It's our job to take care of you. Not the other way around. And it's our privilege and joy to take care of you, Chris."

"I don't know how to be okay with it," I say. "I can't just ignore it. I worry about you guys not having enough money when you're sending so much to me. Or when Ruby ends up in the hospital, or there's anything at home that needs replaced or fixed. I worry about you missing your meds and your treatment. I want to help."

"I know. But you need to focus on your health and wellbeing. On your future." She strokes her fingers through my short curls. "Maybe your father and I haven't been good enough about sharing all the things that family and friends are doing for us already. If we had been sharing those things maybe you wouldn't feel so burdened, my beautiful boy."

I swallow. "Like what?"

"Well, you already know about Mrs. Rodriguez. The woman is a saint and she's also become a wonderful friend. She's helped with transportation, brought meals. Stops in to 'visit' and washes the dishes while she's chatting." Mom grins at that and so do I. "And I think you know about the meals we get from people in the neighborhood and from your father's coworkers. But I guess since my RA diagnosis we've had a lot more support. Stephanie Miller from down the street is coming by in the evenings a couple times a week to help Ruby with her homework. There's a lovely lesbian couple that just moved in across the street who have been using their snow blower to clear our driveway so your father doesn't have to shovel. There's some ladies from church who come by once a week to clean. I have a friend who got me in touch with a few organizations that help people struggling with chronic illness and everything that involves, including finances." She sighs. "It's amazing how long you can be struggling and not know what resources are available to you."

She shakes her head and then says, "And your grandparents help out with medical bills if we really need it. And they volunteer to watch the girls and give us nights out, all expenses paid. Nothing big, but enough to have a meal out if we want, or see a movie. So, yeah, we struggle sometimes, and I'll admit things have gotten harder since I got my RA diagnosis, but the help and support have also gotten bigger. We're not alone, baby, and neither are you."

I have tears sliding down my cheeks again, or maybe they never stopped. She wipes them away. Relief courses through me, because I had no idea they were getting so much help, and it goes a long way to relieve my stress and anxiety. Though I'm always going to worry about Mom's health.

"When you get out of here, we're going to talk about how to get you back on track, okay? No more forty-hour work weeks. No more nights with three or four hours of sleep. You're going to focus on your classes and more self-care. And even though I know it will be hard for you, you are going to let your father and I worry about your father and I. If that means you need to talk to someone then we'll discuss that, too." She kisses my forehead again and squeezes my hand. "I love you so much."

"I love you, too."

She clears her throat and her expression gets more playful. "Now, tell me about that sweet, adorable boy out there who's so obviously in love with you."

PARIS

"Paris, I hope you'll consider joining us for Christmas," Tawnya tells me as we stand outside the airport three weeks later and gather her luggage. Luke had to leave while Chris was still in the hospital so he could get back to work, but he stayed for several days, and it was really nice getting to know both of Chris's parents. It's so easy to see where Chris gets his kindness, compassion, gentleness, and strength.

Tawnya has been at the apartment since Chris was discharged, making sure he was settled and doing okay. She stayed in my room while I shared Chris's, and she gushed over how much she loved my room and my bed canopy, and told me she felt like a princess, which just gave her extra brownie points in my book.

I've been helping Chris shower and dress as much as I can, and Tawnya did some cooking and laundry and washing dishes, though we made sure to tell her over and over not to push herself. She did spend a fair bit of time resting, too, but she also watched TV with us, and helped Chris get back and forth to his classes when I couldn't.

Honestly she's been amazing. She's so sweet and so easy to talk to, and I could tell just how much she loves her son, and vice versa. She's witty and caring, and I'm now following her on Instagram so I get to see all of her amazing art work and share it with everyone I know.

"I'll definitely consider it," I tell her, and I mean it. I love my family and I hate the idea of not being with them over break, but I'm thinking maybe I can split the time, because I hate the thought of not seeing Chris for two weeks either.

"Take care of yourselves," she says, and gives me a hug before she reaches for Chris and embraces him, being careful not to cause him pain. His ribs will need a while longer to heal, as will his wrist, which is currently in a cast, but he's doing better. Mostly because he has been doing a lot of resting since he got home. His headaches and dizziness are gone, and his professors have been really good about making sure he's taking it easy and giving him extra time to complete assignments or have classmates help him with taking notes and stuff, and he hasn't been going to work at all, which has been tough for him, but he told me about the conversation he had with his mom in the hospital and it seemed to help him not be quite as stressed about the financial aspects of things. He and his mom have had a lot of talks in the time she's been here and I think it's been really good for him. It's also been good for him to have time with her to himself.

One of the things that's changed since the accident is that Chris is sharing more with me about how he's feeling, both physically and emotionally, and it means a lot to me that he's confiding in me more and that he feels safe enough to be vulnerable.

"Text me when you get through security," Chris tells his mom. "And as soon as you get on the plane. And when you get home."

It might sound like overkill, but I get why he's so worried. Tawnya doesn't fly alone often because it can be difficult for her, so he wants to make sure she's safe.

"I will," she promises. We wave goodbye and then get back in the car. Chris's hand is on my thigh immediately as I merge onto the interstate and my blood is singing. Our sexual encounters have been a bit limited since his accident. We've shared a few handjobs and I've given him a blow job or two, but we haven't had penetrative sex in weeks and I'm about to lose my mind if I don't get him inside me soon.

The way he's touching me, his hand sliding up my thigh and under my skirt, the way his breath is labored and the fact that I can see his dick tenting his joggers tells me he's just as desperate for me as I am for him.

"Pull over," he says, his voice rough and deep. "I can't wait until we get home. Please, pull over."

My eyes widen, but I do as he asks. As soon as we're on the side of the road and the car is in park he's unbuckling and leaning over the center console, tugging at my skirt. I unbuckle and lift my hips, pulling it down along with my tights and panties.

"Fuck," he growls when he sees my erection and the

precum beaded on my tip. He grips my dick in his hand and strokes me as his mouth meets mine. I whimper and open for him, my body shuddering when he grips my hair and tugs my head back, deepening the kiss and stroking me faster, his grip tightening. When I feel like I'm about to blow he lets go of my cock, but then he's bending over and his mouth is swallowing me down, and it feels so damn good I cry out.

"Fuck, baby." The sounds of my moans and his desperate slurping noises fill the car as his head bobs up and down. It's a little sloppier than normal since one of his hands is incapacitated, but I don't mind at all. His mouth is warm and wet and so fucking perfect. He picks up the pace and I can't stop it. Especially when he moans around my dick like it's the best thing he's ever tasted.

"Chris, fuck," I gasp. And then I'm throwing my head back against the window and releasing inside his mouth with a shout, my body shuddering as he swallows me down. When I catch my breath and open my eyes he's licking his lips, his pupils blown wide. And when I look down I see that his pants are soaked through. Holy shit, he just came untouched in his joggers from blowing me. That's so fucking hot.

He grins and kisses me. "That was just the appetizer," he says. "Let's get home. I want to eat you out and then I want you to ride me. I need your ass so bad, princess."

He pulls his pants down and I see his dick is still hard. "Wait," I say when he reaches for the wipes in the glove box. "Touch yourself. Use your spunk as lube and touch yourself for me. I want to watch."

His gaze heats and he reaches down to grip his cock, slicking it with his spunk as he stares at me. My eyes are riveted to his dick and his hand now stroking slowly up and down. Dear god, I hope we don't get arrested for this, but it might be worth it if we do. My mouth waters as I watch him coat his piercing in his spunk and more precum slides out of that gorgeous slit. He closes his eyes and rests his head back, pleasuring himself slowly, his mouth open and his chest rising and falling.

"Think of how good I'm going to taste, baby," I tell him. "When you have my legs spread and your tongue on me, in me. Think of how good it will feel when we're naked together, how loud I'll be when your fat, gorgeous dick is buried inside me making me feel so damn good."

"Oh, Jesus, Pip." He starts to stroke faster and his hips buck. He's gorgeous and watching him do this is intoxicating. I'm already hard again.

"Picture me in my panties, pulled down around my thighs so you can reach my ass, but you don't want to take them all the way off either. You like the idea of having me mostly naked, but not all the way, and you like seeing my dick straining against them, hard for you, the way it feels to touch me through them, so you leave them around my cock while you eat me and fuck me."

"Oh my god," he gasps, and I can tell he's close. I don't know where all this dirty talk is coming from but I'm obsessed with the way he's responding to it.

"You gonna come for me, baby?" I ask.

"Pip!" he cries out. "Fuck!" His body stiffens and he lets out a deep moan, before his cock spurts rope after rope of cum all over his hand and the front of his jacket. His chest heaves and I can't imagine that feels good on his still sore ribs, but he seems too blissed out at the moment to care.

"Fuck, princess, you have a filthy mouth," he says, turning his head to look at me, a dopey smile on his face.

I blush and grin. Then I'm leaning over the center console and licking the spunk from his dick and his hand.

I pull back onto the interstate after we're both buckled and he's cleaned himself off as best he can. If anything though, I think this little tryst has just made me hornier and the rest of the twenty minute drive home is torture.

I've never moved as quickly as I do once we've pulled into the parking space in front of our building, and we're tearing at each other's clothes the moment the door to the apartment shuts behind us. It's a bit of a struggle getting Chris's shirt off with his cast, but we manage, and then we're kissing fiercely as we move to the bed. I desperately want him to carry me, but that will have to wait until he's healed.

He flops onto his back and lifts his hips. I pull his boxer briefs down and off, tossing them to the floor. Then I'm stripping out of my panties and they follow. "Get on top of me, Pip," he rasps. "I want your ass in my face."

Oh god. I straddle him backwards, which is something I've never done before, and he tugs my hips back so that I'm practically sitting on his face and I get the perfect view of his dick and balls. Then he spreads my cheeks and I moan, my back bowing and my neck arching as he licks over my entrance. I shove my ass back against his tongue and he groans as he feasts on me.

"Oh, oh, oh," I whine, my hips bucking. I shudder when I feel his warm, slick tongue enter me and my cock jerks as precum spills down my shaft and onto his belly. My hands grip his thighs as he tongue fucks me into oblivion.

I'm shaking so hard from the pleasure that I have to grip his legs more firmly to keep from falling off of him.

"You okay?" he asks, his voice rough. I nod my head frantically.

"Yes, fuck, don't stop."

When he resumes his task I take his rock hard dick into my hand and squeeze the base. He grunts and jolts, and then his tongue delves even deeper inside me, making a spark shoot straight to my aching balls.

I lick the tip of his cock over and over, making sure to play with his piercing as I do, and his hips buck. "Oh, fuck, Pip," he groans. "God, that feels amazing." I keep doing it, feeling the way his large hands tighten on my hips and the way he squirms underneath me, his dick oozing precum and twitching with each flick of my tongue over the sensitive slit. He goes back to eating me and I suck the head of his cock into my mouth as he does. We're both moaning obscenely as we pleasure each other and I don't think I've ever been this turned on. I don't want it to stop.

"Oh, fuck, I can't," he gasps, pulling out of me again. "Fuck, Pip, it's too good. I want to be inside you. Please."

I'm loath to lose the sensation of his cock in my mouth and his tongue up my ass, but I also want to feel his dick inside me, buried as far as it will go. I want to fuck myself on him so badly.

I move off of him and straddle him so we're facing each other now. We both groan when our cocks slide together, and then we're kissing again, slow and deep as we touch every inch of each other we can reach.

"Do you want to go without a condom?" he asks once we've stopped for air.

I'm so thrown by the question it takes me a second to answer, and when I do the best I can come up with is, "What?"

He smiles softly and kisses me again. "We could go without a condom if you want. I'm negative and on Prep, and you haven't been with anyone but me. No pressure, but–"

"Yes," I say. "I actually got tested when I started seeing Jeremy just in case." His brows furrow. "Face it, handsome, I had a boyfriend before you. One I never let touch me."

He smirks and I can tell how pleased he is that he's my first everything. My first and my only. I kiss him. "Fuck me bare, baby, I wanna feel you," I tell him.

He kisses me fiercely again and I'm reaching for the lube seconds later. I pop it open and dribble a decent amount on his cock, then start to stroke him. He sucks in a breath when I reach my hand back to slick up my hole. I finger myself briefly, but since he had his tongue inside me for so long I don't need much.

"Fuck, I need you," he pants.

I raise myself up and position his dick under my entrance. Just the pierced tip against my hole has my body thrumming. I let out a breath and slowly start to sink down on him. Holy fucking shit, it's incredible. He's so slick and warm, and that piercing is hitting all the right spots as he enters me.

"Jesus Christ," he groans. "Fuck, Pip, oh my god, you feel so good, princess."

I sink all the way down, and when he's bottomed out inside me I rest my forehead against his. There's a slight burn, but I welcome it. My eyes are closed and my hands rest on either side of him. Fuck, I feel so full, and it's amazing. I kiss him.

"I love you so fucking much."

"I love you, too," he replies. "Now be a good little princess and show me how good you look when you're riding my cock."

That gets my blood pumping all over again and my dick jerks. "Yes, sir."

He growls as he grips my hips and I start to move. It doesn't take long before we have a rhythm going and his piercing is hitting my sweet spot on every rise and fall of my body on his. I'm trying to do most of the work so he doesn't hurt himself, and it's sexy as hell when I grip his arms and hold them over his head as I ride him. I know he could get out of the hold easily, but he doesn't.

"God, you're so damn beautiful, princess," he rasps. "Fuck, your ass is so perfect. Tell me you want me to come inside you."

I whimper at his words and a jolt of electricity races down my spine, making my balls draw up. "I want you to come inside me. I want it so bad, baby. I want you to fill me up and claim me."

He lets out something between a growl and a gasp, and then he's pulling out of my grip and grabbing my dick in his hand. He strokes me as I fuck myself on him and it only takes a few times before I'm shouting and spilling my seed all over his torso, my ass clamping down around him. Seconds later he's groaning and I feel his warmth inside me. It's so good I start to cry.

"You okay?" he asks, and I nod. I lie on top of him for a moment as he strokes my hair, until his dick tells us it's time for him to leave. As soon as he slips out and I roll to my side I feel his spunk sliding down my ass crack and onto my thighs.

Fuck, that's hot.

"Let me see," he says, tapping my thigh. I flush, but move to all fours.

"Holy shit, that's sexy as hell," he says as he kneels behind me, staring at the mess he made. "Damn, Pip, you look good like this."

I wiggle my ass. "You gonna take care of it?"

The next thing I know I feel his tongue sliding along my taint and up to my hole. Then he's licking up the mess on my thighs and letting out a happy hum as he flops back onto his back and takes me in his arms. My mess is still coating his stomach and I run my fingers through it, before bringing it to my lips and sucking it off. Then I rub it into his skin before I reach up and kiss him again.

We lie in silence for a beat before he squeezes me and says, "I think maybe after Christmas I should talk to someone."

I lift my head. "Like a therapist?"

He nods. "I think I could use some help. It scares me, but not talking to someone scares me more, I think. I've just been so stressed for so long I don't know how to not be and I need to figure out some good coping skills, I guess. Talking with Mom helped and I'm not as worried about them as I was, but I need more. I need to figure out how to have a better balance in my life."

"I'm really proud of you," I tell him. "I do think it's a good idea. You deserve to feel better and I think a therapist can help with that."

He nods. "The nurse at the hospital suggested yoga once I can actually move around a little more again. I know about meditation, and I should start exercising again. I did it a lot more before I got my job and it was good for me." He takes a breath and lets it out. "I also think I'm depressed and haven't really recognized it for what it is until now."

"That makes sense," I tell him. "With everything you're dealing with and how burned out you are." I rest my hand on his chest and look into his warm brown eyes. "I'm here for you, no matter what. I'll do yoga with you if you want. It could be fun. I don't run unless someone is chasing me, though."

He laughs and presses a kiss to my lips. "Thank you for being so patient with me. So understanding. It means a lot that you are sticking with me through all of this."

"It's not even a choice, baby. I'd do anything for you. And I know you would do anything for me."

"I know. I know you would."

TWENTY-FIVE

PARIS

"Hey, I'm really glad you came," Chris says as he wraps his arms around me at the baggage claim of the Minneapolis-St.Paul International airport. The hug is bulky since we're both bundled in winter gear, but we manage.

It's three days after Christmas and I've missed him so much I can't stand it. Sure we talked and Face-Timed while we were each with our families over break, and I loved seeing my parents and spending more time with my brother and Jackson, but being away from Chris was painful.

"Me, too," I say.

I'm about to kiss him when I hear, "Hi, I'm Ruby." I look to my left to see a young girl, who I know now is Chris's little sister, beaming at me. She has a bright orange hat on over her dark brown curls, and her skin is light brown just like Chris, but her eyes are green. She holds her hand out to me and I shake it.

"Nice to meet you, Ruby, I'm Paris."

"She insisted on coming to pick you up," Chris tells me, looking a little sheepish, but also like he would do anything to indulge her and doesn't actually mind. "And Dad was coming anyway since I still can't drive because of my ribs, so it's a whole family affair."

I laugh. "Sounds fun. Where is your dad?"

"He dropped us off and is circling the pick up zone."

"Woah, that's your suitcase?" Ruby asks when she sees the large bright pink luggage I pull off the baggage claim.

"It is. Pink is my favorite color."

"I like pink, but my favorite color is orange. Can I pull it?"

"It's kinda heavy," I tell her.

"I'm tough," she insists. "Come on, hand it over."

I do and Chris smiles at me. We make our way to the sliding glass doors that lead out to the pick up zone and Chris calls his dad to tell him where we are. A minute later their car pulls up and Luke climbs out, taking the suitcase from Ruby and hefting it into the trunk.

"That's a big suitcase, baby," Chris teases.

"Are you kidding, do you know how much stuff I left behind? That's packing light for me." I stand on my tiptoes and whisper in his ear. "I brought plenty of panties though." I grin when I feel him shiver against me.

His eyes sparkle and he pecks me on the cheek. It's freezing cold out here, and when Ruby tells me to climb in the backseat with her I don't hesitate.

"How are you doing, Paris?" Luke asks as we pull into traffic. "Did you have a good Christmas?"

"Yeah, I did, thank you. And thank you for having me. I'm excited to be here."

"Well, we're excited to have you."

"They made us clean the whole house," Ruby chimes in, and I laugh. "Mom made me do the toilets because apparently I'm old enough now." She makes a face and I laugh again.

"I know what that's like." I wish I could sit next to Chris and hold his hand since they tell me it's a two hour drive to Princeton where they live. But I'll survive.

"So, Paris," Ruby says, folding her hands primly on her lap and looking over at me. "Tell me about yourself."

"What do you want to know?"

"Everything."

So we drive and I talk, and every once in a while Luke asks me a question, too, about my home, my parents, my interests. Chris is fairly quiet and just absorbing it all. I can see him smiling from where I'm sitting diagonally to him.

It hardly even seems like it's been two hours when we pull up to the home Chris grew up in. It's a two story, with light blue paint in a quiet neighborhood. A little bit older build, but well kept, and of course the yard is covered in snow. There's Christmas lights on the roof and over the garage, and some Christmas decorations in the yard as well. A couple of reindeer grazing and a few presents that all light up, and you can see their Christmas tree through the second story window. Chris has a smile on his face when he tells me their neighbors got together to put the lights up for them since his dad was busy and his mom wasn't feeling well.

Ruby insists on hauling my suitcase inside once Luke gets it out of the trunk and we walk up the porch and into the house. It's warm and it smells like evergreen and cinnamon.

The house is split level so there's stairs leading up as soon as you enter and stairs leading down. The living area is directly to the left up the stairs and the kitchen/dining are straight ahead.

"Take your shoes off and I'll give you the tour," Chris says. "Ruby, can you put Paris's suitcase in my room?"

I flush, but Ruby picks up the suitcase and clomps down the stairs. "Is she going to be able to manage that?" I ask.

"She's stronger than I am," Chris says. "She'll be fine."

We go up the stairs first, into the kitchen. There's a back door leading out to a raised deck that overlooks the ample yard and the house behind theirs. We don't go out there because it's freezing and covered in snow, but I get the view from inside the warm kitchen.

There's cinnamon rolls on the counter and a box of chocolate chip cookies. "Hungry?" Chris asks with a chuckle when I eye them.

"Starving, actually."

"Grab one. You can eat while we walk. Dad will make dinner soon."

I snatch a cinnamon roll because they look absolutely delicious and take a huge bite out of it. "God, these are amazing. Who made them?"

He grins. "I did. I've done a lot of baking since I've been home. I'm realizing how much it helps me relax."

I smile wide. "I love that." I kiss him and we continue with the tour. We spot who I assume is Janelle in the living room, curled up in an armchair, looking at her phone.

"Janelle, this is Paris," Chris says. I'm honestly surprised when she puts her phone down to say hello to me.

"Hey, what's up?" she says. "My brother won't shut up about you." She winks at him and his skin takes on a slight flush. He reaches for my hand and squeezes. "I hope you like board games because this family is big on them and we don't show mercy."

I grin. "I'm up for anything."

"Also I love your makeup. And your skirt. They give major Barbie."

I beam. "Thank you."

"Is Mom in her room?" Chris asks, and she nods.

"She's okay. Just resting. She had a long day."

He nods and tugs me down the hall. To the right just past the living room is a bathroom. To the left is a room with the door closed and I can hear soft voices on the other side. I'm assuming it's his parents' room. Straight ahead is another room, and when Chris opens the door and turns the light on, my mouth almost drops. It must be Tawnya's art studio because it's covered in paint, easels, canvases, drop cloths on the floor, and there's shelving and drawers for storage filled with various brushes and paints. There's a few lamps positioned throughout the room, and there's even a section that looks like it's set up for taking pictures of the work when it's finished.

It smells like cleaners and earth, and it's lovely. I love that I get to see this, that Chris is sharing this with me.

"This is incredible," I say. My eyes fall on a canvas that has what looks like the beginnings of a country landscape, with the barn in the background and a gorgeous creek running through the land. It's stunning. I can see why Chris is having a hard time with his mom not being healthy enough to paint as often as she used to. I mean, I understood before, but this puts it in a little bit more perspective. It would be hard to see this room empty when you are used to it being so full of life.

"Is it hard, her not being in here?"

"Yeah, sometimes. But I have to remind myself that even when she can't work she's still an artist and an amazing human being, and that I get to call her Mom, which is pretty incredible. I'll never understand why she has to deal with what she does, or be glad she's sick. But I think that when you have so many difficult moments it makes the good moments more special in a way. And we hold on to that. Lots of families wouldn't think it's a big deal if their Mom was able to paint for a few hours, or wash dishes, or vacuum, or play a game, or bake something with her kids, or make it to a soccer game or a Christmas concert, but those are the things that are big for us. The things that matter most."

I let him tug me to his side and squeeze me. I squeeze him back, wrapping my arms around his waist. He presses a kiss to my curls. "Thank you for sharing this with me. For sharing your family with me. It means a lot."

We move downstairs next, where there's a smaller living area with a TV set up and some video game consoles. To the left is Ruby's room, and he lets me peek inside, until Ruby shoots off of her bed and takes my hand, yanking me in. She spends the next several minutes showing me her favorite plushies, her *K-Pop Demon Hunters* dolls, which honestly are pretty cool, her soccer trophies and medals, which I'm super impressed by because I can't play sports to save my life, though I did enjoy being on cheer team in high school, and when I tell her as much she insists I do a cheer for her.

Of course I do even though it makes me blush fiercely, but Chris is smiling so wide the whole time I don't regret it at all.

Janelle's room is also down here, as well as a laundry room, bathroom, and at the end of the hall, Chris's room. It's bigger than the other two, with a full sized oak bed, dresser, and nightstand. There's a small desk in the corner with a laptop on it, and two large windows draped by navy blue curtains. There's some sports posters on the walls, basketball, football, along with different musicians including Tracy Chapman, Brandi Carlile, and Tina Turner. On his desk sits a photo of his family, and there's a pride flag above his desk as well that makes me smile.

I pick up the photo and grin at a younger Chris, probably fifteen or sixteen. Lean and tall, the same short, curly hair and wide smile. No scruff yet like he has now. Different, but just as beautiful.

"I'm going to need to see way more photos of younger Chris," I tell him.

"Later," he says, taking the frame from me gently and setting it back on his desk. "I'm sure Mom would love nothing more than to break out my baby book."

He closes the door and locks it, before he tugs me to the bed. We lie down and make out for a while, our hands roaming.

"Have I told you how glad I am that you're here?" he asks.

"You have. But I love hearing it."

There's a knock on the door about fifteen minutes later and then Ruby's voice. "You guys aren't being icky are you? No smooching."

We laugh.

"What is it, Ruby?" Chris asks.

"Dinner will be ready soon. And Mom is up."

Chris rolls off the bed and I follow him.

When we get upstairs, Janelle is setting the table while Luke stands over the portable grill. Tawnya stands from her seat in the living room and walks over to me. She embraces me and gives me a warm smile.

"It's so good to see you again, sweetie," she says.

"Let's eat," Luke calls, and we gather around the table. Dinner is grilled chicken, mashed potatoes, and salad and it looks delicious. My stomach growls and Ruby giggles.

"Eat as much as you want," Luke tells me with a smile.

We start passing the food around and then there's talk about what game we'll be playing after dinner.

There's laughter and warmth and so much love I feel like my heart can't contain it. And of course there's bickering too, because what else would you expect with ten and fourteen year olds.

Janelle gets told to put her phone away at the table and rolls her eyes, but obeys. Ruby talks about how excited she is for Luke to take her sledding tomorrow. Tawnya asks how my Christmas was. I tell her Chris showed me her art studio and how amazing it is. She says she made a few extra sales in December which is really nice and I tell her I've been spreading the word about her work.

"That's so sweet of you," she says. "Thank you."

We end up playing Yahtzee and then Uno, after which Tawnya says she needs to lie down.

Later that night we watch *Elf* together, eating yummy snacks and sipping on hot chocolate.

Over the next several days Chris and I watch quite a few movies with his family, several episodes of *The Good Place*, play lots of games, and spend time baking. We also do some yoga, which I'm realizing I like quite a bit and it does seem to help Chris, too.

Tawnya joins in for most of the indoor activities, and Chris and I stay home with her when the rest of the family goes ice skating. We make and frost sugar cookies and Tawnya visits with us while we do. Luke forgets his lunch one day so Chris and I drive it to the garage where he works and we get to meet his coworkers.

I get to see all the baby pictures of Chris, and Tawnya can't stop telling me stories. We watch the videos his parents took of some of Ruby's soccer games, including the one where she broke her arm, and Janelle's choir concerts, and let me tell you that girl can sing.

One of my favorite parts of being here is meeting the support system Chris's family is surrounded by. I've met several of the neighbors as well and they are so sweet and kind.

My other favorite part is watching Tawnya and Luke dancing to Tracy Chapman or Sean Mendez after dinner each night before Tawnya goes to rest, and especially the first time when Chris takes my hand and starts dancing with me, too.

Ruby gags and runs away and we all laugh, while Janelle rolls her eyes and smiles.

Being with Chris and watching him with his family is making me realize just how much happier he is when he's home. He's less stressed and tense, and I can't imagine how hard it's been for him to be away for so long.

"Have you been applying to grad schools out here?" I ask one night as we lie in bed after sucking each other off (quietly).

"Yeah, a couple, but I kind of have to go where I get a scholarship, if that's still an option now. And I don't think I could go to school out here and have you in Colorado."

"You'll get a scholarship. I know you will."

"Thanks, Pip. We'll see." He kisses my hair as I snuggle against him. I know how much it means to him to get into grad school and I want that for him more than anything. I really think he can do it if he's cutting back on work hours and focusing on his classes. He's brilliant and he's going to make an amazing PT. But I also hate the idea of him being so far away from his family for another several years.

"If you do get accepted somewhere in Minnesota, I could come with you."

His hand stills from where it's been stroking my spine. I look at him. "I mean it. I would follow you anywhere, but especially here, so you can be with your family. You deserve that. And there's no way I'm letting you go to school out of state without me. I'm in this for the long haul."

His eyes are soft when he speaks. "You would do that for me? Leave your family and friends, and school, and follow me out here?"

Would it be hard? Yeah, of course. But he's been away from home long enough and I will still see my family. I mean, over Christmas and summer, and maybe even spring break. Chris could come with me or not depending on what his schedule is like. I don't know, I just know we could figure it out. I can't expect him to stay in Colorado forever when his heart is here. "Yeah," I say. "Yeah, I would."

"You might resent me if you realized it was harder than you thought. I would never forgive myself if that happened."

I shake my head. "I could never resent you for a choice I made. I love my family, but I love you, too. I like change. I like trying new things and having new experiences and meeting people. And I love your family and your neighbors and the community you have here. We could visit Colorado at least once a year, and my parents and Preston could come out here and visit us. We'd get sick of them."

He gives me a soft smile. "Let's see what happens, huh?"

I kiss him. "I love you more than anything."

"Love you, too, princess."

CHRIS

A month after Christmas is over I'm finally feeling like I've gotten back on my feet a little bit. My body is healed from the accident for the most part, I've cut my work hours down to half time so I can focus more on school and get more sleep, and it's already making a difference in my grades. And the yoga and running each morning is helping too.

But I'm still struggling, and my knee bounces up and down as I sit in the small waiting room. I'm too nervous to look at my phone so my gaze roams the room. There's a couch, two chairs, and some artificial plants decorating the space as well as different pamphlets on depression, anxiety, OCD, and more. There's floral artwork and motivational quotes decorating the off white walls.

When the door opens a few minutes later, a tall blonde woman steps out, probably in her late thirties, dressed in slacks, a purple blouse, and heels. She has her hair pulled back in a pony tail and she smiles when she sees me.

"Chris?"

I nod and she holds her hand out. "Hi. I'm Dr. Valerie Prescot. It's nice to meet you."

EPILOGUE

SIX YEARS LATER

PARIS

Everyone claps as I blow out the big "Twenty Five" candle on my very pink birthday cake and Chris pecks a kiss to my cheek. I couldn't be happier. Everyone is here to celebrate the occasion. My parents, Preston and Jackson, Vanessa and Trent. All of them flew to Minnesota to be here for me. And of course Chris's family is here as well, in our little two bedroom apartment only a fifteen minute drive from his parents' place.

We moved in a couple of months ago and we'll be here for the foreseeable future.

Chris did get a scholarship but he waited a year after undergrad to apply. After everything his senior year he still needed to take things slow. In the meantime he used his undergrad degree to teach physical education at the nearby middle school as well as doing some personal training on the side.

He is officially a PT as of two years ago, and he loves it. He loves helping people regain their quality of life and working with people of all ages and backgrounds. And the best part for him is that he's been able to help his mom in a tangible way that doesn't leave him feeling stressed, depleted, or exhausted.

Leaving Colorado was hard, I won't lie, but honestly it wasn't as hard as I thought it might be. I love living near Chris's family and I love the friends I've made. I enrolled in a nearby college when I first got here, and when I was finished with my undergrad I applied to grad school so I could get my masters degree in counseling, which I'm in my second year of since I'm part-time, and I'm super excited about getting out there eventually and helping people in my own way, particularly the queer community.

I do miss my friends. Trent and Vanessa weren't happy when they heard I was following Chris to Minnesota, but they understood and have been supportive. We talk several times a week on FaceTime and keep each other updated on school, life, and relationships. And they've been out to visit me several times. My parents struggled, especially Mom, but she knew I had to do it to be with Chris and she and Dad are elated that the two of us are together. They've always adored Chris.

Preston visits at least twice a year, and I've been back for holidays and special events as much as I can, and I bring Chris with me as much as possible. Since seeing family and friends is so important for us we have a budget for exactly that. I think it's an essential part of our self-care just like so many other things.

I don't know what the future holds of course, but I do know I want all of these people in my life even if we're not seeing each other on a regular basis.

Ginger, my beautiful sweet girl, passed away a few months after Christmas my freshman year. We were still living in Colorado at the time and Chris and I drove home so I could see her one last time and say my goodbyes. Dad says she went quietly, snuggled on his lap in front of the fireplace. I was a wreck of course, even though I knew it was coming. She held on for almost seventeen years and had such a special place in my heart, in all our hearts, and saying goodbye to someone you love never gets easier.

Chris was amazing as always. He held me as I sobbed like a baby, listened to all my family's stories as we remembered her and how much joy she brought us. Even sat with me and looked through all the pictures we had of her from the moment we brought her home as a puppy.

Then Chris surprised me with the sweetest gift a couple of weeks later. He got me a coffee mug with a few different pictures of Ginger on it, and underneath the words "Dogs leave pawprints on our hearts." Of course I sobbed all over again, but I use it every day and it makes missing her a little easier.

Chris was in therapy for a while and while he still struggles with not feeling responsible for his family's well-being sometimes and worries about his mom in general, he's doing much better. Fortunately Dr. Prescot, his therapist, is licensed in Minnesota so he was still able to see her after he graduated college. He just had to do virtual visits. She was super helpful, working with him to develop better coping mechanisms for his stress. She coached him on grounding techniques, setting boundaries and saying when he is struggling or needs something. She helped him learn to identify unhealthy thought patterns, and encouraged him to focus on the things in his life he can control, rather than what he can't. She taught him to prioritize self care and take breaks. And she mentioned a few non-profits that his parents hadn't heard of before that might be able to help Chris's mom with her health expenses and provide support on top of the ones her friend told her about. And we set aside a small amount of money every month just in case they need it or we want to spoil them with something special like a getaway of some kind, but he doesn't work himself to the bone. Living so close to home the past several years has helped a lot, too.

I'm so damn proud of him, and I remind him of that every day. Just like he reminds me every day how much he loves me and that he's proud to be with me. He's happier and healthier and it shows.

I grin when he feeds me my first bite of birthday cake while everyone watches like it's our wedding, and then he kisses me.

When he moves to pull away I grip his cheeks and kiss him harder. I don't have a clue where the road will lead us, but I know I want this man with me on the journey, through all the bumps, all the valleys and hills, all the sunrises and sunsets.

I want to be his princess and for him to be my prince every single day for the rest of forever. He is the choice I will make over and over again no matter what. Loving him and being loved by him is my greatest adventure, and a lifetime together will never be enough.

"Happy birthday, princess," he murmurs against my lips, a wide smile on his handsome face. "I love you so damn much."

"I love you, too," I tell him. "My handsome prince."

The End

Thank you for reading Chris and Paris's story. If you enjoyed it please consider leaving a review. You can find the paperback and hardcover versions on Amazon as well as my payhip website, Barnes and Noble, Books a Million, and more!

You can follow me on social media, join my Facebook group, sign up for my newsletter, and find the rest of my books here: https://linktr.ee/felsnowauthor